Life is What You Make it

Preeti Shenoy is an author and artist based in Bangalore, India. Her first book *34 Bubblegums and Candies*, a creative non-fiction, made it to the national bestseller list.

Her interests are as multifarious and diverse as her several academic degrees. She also specialises in pencil portraits and holds an internationally recognised qualification from UK in portraiture. She has held a number of varied jobs in the past. She has also written for different publications like *Reader's Digest* and *The Times of India*, as well as taught English and Math to underprivileged children in India. She loves art, reading, travelling, photography, nature, animals, blogging, basketball, and most of all, spending time with her spouse and two children.

Praise for Preeti Shenoy's earlier book:

"A simple narration with umpteen smart phrases makes the book a one session reading."

—***The Times of India***

"Sharp observations that cut close to the bone, witticisms that encapsulate honest-to-goodness home truths, not to forget musings of a keenly observant mind."

—***DNA***

"Easy to read lucid style. The mundane and quotidian turns into great literary stuff in the hands of the author."

—***Deccan Herald***

"This book promises to be a show stealer."

—***Deccan Chronicle***

Life is What You Make it

A story of love, hope and how determination can overcome even destiny

Preeti Shenoy

Srishti
PUBLISHERS & DISTRIBUTORS

Srishti Publishers & Distributors
Registered Office: N-16, C.R. Park
New Delhi – 110 019
Corporate Office: 212A, Peacock Lane
Shahpur Jat, New Delhi – 110 049
editorial@srishtipublishers.com

First published by
Srishti Publishers & Distributors in 2011

117

Printed and bound in India

For Satish, Atul and Purvi,
without them I am nothing.
For Dad and Mom who give me strength.
For my closest friends Ajay and Cherissa
who accept me as I am.

INVICTUS

William Ernest Henley

Out of the night that covers me,
Black as the Pit from pole to pole,
I thank whatever gods may be
For my unconquerable soul.

In the fell clutch of circumstance
I have not winced nor cried aloud.
Under the bludgeonings of chance
My head is bloody, but unbowed.

Beyond this place of wrath and tears
Looms but the Horror of the shade,
And yet the menace of the years
Finds and shall find me unafraid.

It matters not how strait the gate,
How charged with punishments the scroll,
I am the master of my fate;
I am the captain of my soul.

Prologue

I wait my turn on the chair outside the doctor's office. The psychiatrist, to be precise. The so-called expert. We have travelled all the way from Bombay to Bangalore to make this trip. Getting an appointment here is like getting an appointment to meet the Pope at the Vatican City. I don't know how many months one has to wait to get an appointment for that. I am told many months. For this visit, dad had to pull a whole lot of strings. Finally one of his oldest friends managed to get it. It is one of the best mental health care centres in India. Or so I have been told. Perhaps it is. Every magazine and every newspaper seems to mention it and quote its expert doctors on anything to do with mental health.

The drive to this place itself is beginning to seem ominous. The road lined with large trees, spreading their branches covering the place with gloom, as our hired car makes its way, it makes me want to get down and run. But I do no such thing. I sit and watch my surroundings. There is a blue board with large white letters proclaiming the name of the mental health institute, which is spread over a sprawling campus of ten acres, full of old buildings with fading yellow paint, dingy corridors, trees, bushes even a cafeteria and scores of vehicles in which patients arrive with their families in search of hope. In me, there is none left. There is only despondency and an increasing feeling of frustration.

We pass a large building brandishing a board which proclaims it is some kind of a guest house. I notice the peeling paint again. The car passes the other buildings, the Psychiatry ward, the Casualty and Emergency services, the De-addiction centre, the General ward, the Observation ward and the pale yellow cottages called units for some in-house patients. It looks like any other hospital and there is nothing to suggest that it is a mental hospital, except of course if you observe the signs and the people. I hate it all. It fills me with a kind of dread. I don't belong here. I ought not to even be here in the first place. But I am, and there is nothing I can do about it.

The driver parks the car and we enter a building which is an out-patient screening block. It has more than a hundred people and their families, all waiting. The faint stench of human odour which emanates when bodies are packed together, hits my nostril and I hold my breath involuntarily. My dad approaches the counter and joins the serpentine queue which seems to be inching forward at the pace of a snail and I read the board at the entrance on which the following is written in bold letters:

"Patients visiting National Mental Health Institute for the first time are requested to register themselves at this block for consultation/ treatment.

Registration is carried out between 8:00 A.M and 11:00 A.M on all days except Sundays and certain specific holidays.

Please observe queue."

I realize with a sinking feeling that the patient now refers to me. I feel helpless. I feel lost. I feel angry.

And in my mind I think that the whole mental health institute thing is bull shit. Hype. They talk nonsense and have no clue as to what they are doing or saying. I don't want to be here. I don't want to see any psychiatrist or doctor. My opinion now does not matter anymore. I had my chance and I screwed it up badly. Now I have no choice except to listen to my parents and go along with whatever they suggest. So much for my attempts at being independent. So much for my attempts at being an adult.

I sit between my mother and father. I feel like a kid but I am 21, a full grown adult. At least technically. The chair is made of metal and feels cold. I try to hide the scars on my wrist, and adjust the broad leather strap of my watch, out of habit. Curious stares and worse, the looks of pity irk me. I don't want any of it. Especially, not now. Especially, not today. I don't regret my past actions at all. Physical pain is far easier to bear than mental agony. To be really honest, if I had another chance I think I would do it again. I look at the anguish on my dad's face and the look of constant worry on my mother's brow, just like those unwanted notices stuck on the roadside walls. I don't feel sorry for them at all, though I am supposed to be. I don't even wish I could erase them. I don't want to comfort them or make them feel better. I am helpless. Beyond caring. I don't give a damn. I want it all to end. I don't want to see yet another doctor. I am tired of it all. What is this doctor going to tell me that others haven't?

I loathe them all. The whole lot of them. They know nothing. My face is expressionless. I am incapable of feeling empathy. It is as though my heart has turned to wood. Rotting, festering wood that gnaws at the core of my being and threatens to drag me in. I was not like this. But that was then and this is now.

I look at the other patients waiting their turns outside. There are at least one hundred and sixty or maybe more. The waiting room is actually a long cavernous hall about fifty feet by thirty feet and there are iron chairs arranged in rows, one behind the other. It seems like the waiting room at a railway station and just as crowded too. There is a guy sitting on the chair with his arms round his legs, rocking back and forth, back and forth. There is a girl who looks around my age staring listlessly outside. "I am not like you. I won elections in my college. I used to be the Secretary of the Arts Association. I was doing my management from a fine business school. I am not like you all." I want to scream at all of them. I want to tell them that I am a somebody , at least in my world which consists of college, home, friends, fun, movies—the normal world, not this hospital where people who cannot cope come to seek help. I am 'educated', superior, knowledgeable, and smart. The pathetic, helpless situation that I am finding myself in is somehow making me want to prove that I am better than all of them. But it feels like somebody has stuffed a cloth in my mouth to prevent me from talking. I am unable to say anything. At the back of my mind I also realize that in reality, maybe I am in no way better than them. I am a nobody. Here I am just a patient, waiting in turn with scores of others, waiting simply to see the doctor.

My gaze becomes transfixed on a middle aged man who cannot stop making small circulatory motions with his thumb. The air is dry, suffocating and oppressive. Outside, it is bright but shady. The psychiatrist inside will assess me and decide the next course of action

What does he know? Can he look into my head? Does he even know what I am going through? Does medical school teach you to feel another's pain or step into their shoes? Most of the doctors I have spoken to are impersonal and clinical. They are trained to be so. I highly doubt if this one is going to be any different.

Eventually, the nurse calls out my patient number. No one gives a damn about my name or what I used to be. I rise to enter his office. So do my parents. The doctor speaks to us. My dad is explaining my 'symptoms'. I wince. That is not how it is, I want to scream. But I don't want them to think that I am out of control. So I dig my finger nails into my skin to prevent me from talking. I grit my teeth and listen. The doctor asks my dad and mom to wait outside.

Then he looks at me. He looks nice. He is young. He seems kind but that does not fool me. He is just a professional asshole being paid to assess me. I decide to co-operate. It is the best way.

Then he starts asking questions. I detest someone prying into my life like this. I hate having to go through all this, again.

He starts off with mundane questions. Childhood, School, College. I look at him dully. I don't feel like telling him anything.

"Look," he says. "I need to enter all this info here. Do you want to tell me or do you want me to ask your parents?"

I feel trapped, cornered, exasperated and suddenly very tired. I just want it to end.

So I start to answer.

1

A new world

1989

July 3rd

Cochin

Dear Vaibhav,

I am really happy that you have got into IIT-D.

Why can't parents be a bit more understanding? How I wish I could study in Delhi. I know I can easily get into LSR with my academic record. What fun will it be to hang out together!

But my mother says no. My dad seconds her. They want me to study here.

The college is not really bad. It is the best in the state and the oldest too. It is a matter of prestige if you get in here. My parents have not stopped boasting to anyone who will listen that I have got into St. Agnes. It will start a week's time.

I miss our gang in school. I wish my dad had not got a transfer here. We could still have been together then.

Take care

Ankita

1989

July 9th

Delhi

Dearest Ankita,

We have to accept the things that we cannot change. I miss you a lot.

I got your letter just now and I am replying immediately.

My orientation is tomorrow. I am excited! I cannot believe I am an IITian now! I love the campus, the hostel and everything else.

I tried calling you. But your mother hung up on me. Looks like I will have to wait for your letters. It reaches me only on the 5th day of your posting it. Five days is so long! But it is better than nothing I guess.

Do tell me how you like your college. It must have started by the time my letter reaches you.

Luv

Vaibhav

Before the advent of the Internet or computers, we wrote letters by hand and waited eagerly for the postman to deliver one. Those were the days of epic television drama serials like *Buniyaad* and programmes *Chitrahaar,* when television meant just one national channel and when video cassette recorders were still in vogue.

Looking back I am surprised. Given how conservative, strict *and* Indian my parents were, they actually allowed me to write letters to a boy, considering the fact that I was not permitted to invite boys home or to visit any boy's house, even if I was with a group of girls. When my gang consisting of four boys and three girls, were going out for a movie and for ice-creams later, after my class 12 Board Exams, I was the only one not permitted to go. Perhaps, they let me write letters as no one would *see* them whereas going out for a movie or ice creams meant that people would *see* and they would talk.

The first feeling I had when I entered the college gates was that of breathlessness. I had hurried to make it in time for the first day at college. I could not believe that my school days were actually over and I was officially a college student.

No more school uniforms. No more strict rules. No more being treated as a kid. I would be 18 on my next birthday and officially an adult. I felt excited as legally it meant I was eligible to marry and vote. The flip side immediately struck me too. I would no longer be a juvenile and could be arrested too. Of course, at that time I had no idea how dangerously close I'd come to it. It was an exhilarating feeling—like a caterpillar emerging out of a cocoon. I could hardly wait.

It would take at least twenty pages of writing to describe my college to Vaibhav.

The buildings were smart, modern and pristinely clean. There was a solitary tree in the middle of the courtyard, standing proudly, on which hung a bell. A circular platform went around the tree and some students were sitting on it, some standing, and all chattering excitedly. The bell would be rung throughout the day to indicate the end of a period.

The campus area was about five acres and the building had expanded vertically. There were three wings— the old, the new and the hostels. The old wing had spellbinding architecture and I gazed at its beautiful arches. This wing also housed the very large, well equipped library spread over three floors, the administrative offices and the principal's office, apart from the various counters for collecting forms, paying fees and other things associated with an academic institution. Four spotless wooden showcases with crystal clear glass proudly displayed the gleaming, glittering trophies that Agnites had won over the past eighty years. The trophies spilled over to two deep brown rosewood antique tables too. It instilled in me a kind of awe and respect, something similar to what one feels when one enters a building that belongs to the Armed forces in the country. It was a very positive and vibrant feeling. I could even see my reflection in the polished wood.

The auditorium was large and easily accommodated all the students. The stage was done up with élan and there was the college logo, a huge crest which proclaimed the motto of the college with pride. The audio system, the speakers and the whole set up was very impressive. So was the Principal of the college, a nun named Sister Evangeline who welcomed us in perfect English, telling us about the college, its history, its achievement, its vision, its aim and the high standards expected of each Agnite. I began to feel pride slowly stirring in me.

Never in my life had I seen so many women or girls in one place. Throughout my life I had studied in co-educational schools where men were a part of my world. Suddenly being thrust into an atmosphere without any, had taken me completely by surprise Everywhere I turned, looked or went it was women, women and more women. The college must have had at least three thousand students and it seemed as if almost all of them had turned up at the college auditorium for the welcome and induction at the start of the new academic year. I remember staring in wonder and thinking that it meant 6000 breasts and 3000 vaginas were in the auditorium. I smiled to myself at my wicked thought.

I looked forward eagerly to the classes that would begin soon.

2

Nothings gonna stop us now

How do groups get formed in colleges? Some say that you gravitate instinctively towards people you can relate to and then gradually over the months a bond develops.

It was not like that with my class. It felt as though a snooker player had hit a single hard strike and we, like the snooker balls, had scattered in all directions, random balls coming together with no pre-determined plan. But of course, in reality, each shot is planned with precision and each strike is made with a purpose, and on deeper contemplation you realize that the balls came together for a reason after all.

Almost instantly we had gravitated towards a gang or a group. There were sixty of us but we had all fallen into our groups, with whom we hung out, exchanged notes and had fun with. Mine was a group of four. Apart from me, there was Suvi, Janie and Charu.

Suvi undoubtedly had the most dynamic personality in the group. She was short but what she lacked in height she made up in other areas. She was smart, stylish and enthusiastic with an attitude that was contagious. Most people warmed up to her. She was a bundle of energy, always ready for anything, a little impulsive and reckless too at times.

Charu, a Tam-brahm, was a personification of the generalizations that are made about them. She was studious, smart and intelligent. She even wore glasses. Her aim was to become a chartered accountant.

Janie was the gentle, quiet and the sensible one. Her ambition was either to become a nun or do her MSW and take up social work. We came together like a patchwork quilt and got along well despite our very different personalities.

But what I did not expect to learn so quickly at college was the 'Great-Agnes-embarrass-a-guy- by-staring- at- his-crotch' tradition. We were introduced, instructed and inducted into it by our seniors when we shared a lecture with them for Mercantile Law, which was the only subject in the whole college being taught by a male. The raging hormones plus the losing of all inhibitions that a woman's college does to you, was enough for everyone to co-operate on the single point agenda of this tradition. He was nick named Porukki-merki. '*Porruki*' was a colloquial word in the local language. Loosely translated it stood for an oaf or a 'good-for-nothing' guy, implying he was a skirt chaser. Which was really ironic as it were the girls who were doing the pretend-chase here, not him.

The girls mostly stared very pointedly at his crotch throughout the duration of the lecture. He would begin by pretending not to notice. But of course, he would notice. There was no way he could not see something as obvious and outrageous as that, but he couldn't do a thing. The unspoken rule was that in Mercantile Law Class, you were allowed only to look at Merki's crotch. There were about a hundred and twenty of us, women, all starved of male company and his looks did not deter us at all. Merki was a middle aged, short, slightly overweight professor, with pot belly and he always tucked his shirt in. He had a large mop of thick black, oily, curly head and a moustache shaped like the head of a toilet cleaning brush. His eyes were tiny black slits on his chubby face and they darted quickly in all directions. He could have been a bad caricature of a hero of a Malayalam movie. He would begin by explaining some concept in Mercantile Law earnestly and then within ten minutes, beads of sweat would begin appearing on his forehead. He would then take out his spotless white handkerchief and mop his brow repeatedly. The girls were relentless. Even when he asked a question, the girl who stood up to answer would still not take her eyes away from his crotch. I really pitied the poor man. But secretly I wondered if he actually enjoyed it too. I doubted if he ever got any female attention outside the gates of the college.

My letters to Vaibhav described all this and more. Our letters to each other were getting longer and longer. We became experts in anticipating how much postage would be needed for each letter. As the weeks sped our letters to each other were our constant connection, our link and the happiness we derived from them kept both of us going.

During the day, in the middle of some activity I was busily involved in, I caught myself thinking of something he had written and I found myself smiling. I caught myself making mental notes to tell him about little things that had just occurred. He wrote that it was the same for him. He said he never remembered being so enthusiastic about life, before this. He said I gave him an anchor, a purpose and a meaning to his existence. I told him he was a sentimental fool and he should write poetry. Secretly of course, I loved it. He knew it too. I liked being adored. I liked the feeling of being so important to someone. I liked being the centre of someone's world.

A year flew by and I did not even feel it pass. Then when my 18th birthday was approaching, he decided that letters were just not enough. He said he wanted to talk to me.

Getting to talk to Vaibhav on the phone involved putting together a complex combat mission much like U.S Airborne division of paratroopers in World War Two. There were no mobile phones those days. It required detailed, precise planning, a lot of forethought and co-ordination down to the last detail. He had once tried the direct approach and called up at a decent hour. My mother had answered the phone. He greeted her and she had said a curt 'Yes?' She did not return the greeting. She said "Ankita cannot come to the phone right now" and had hung up abruptly. I was in my room and had heard every word. My ears burnt with indignation and tears of anger were swelling in my eyes. But I hid them well. There was no way I could argue with her.

That did not stop us though. We both agreed that a phone call would be considered successful if we managed to speak to each other for at least four minutes. Vaibhav had outlined three parts for '**Operation Mission Phone-call.**'

Part one was **Pre mission planning considerations** which were

1. My brother had to be asleep.

2. My parents had to be out for their morning walk which they usually never missed.

Part two was **Support forces** which were

1. The telephone booth guy from where Vaibhav made those early

morning phone calls should have woken up. (Vaibhav later told me that he had to shake him vigorously or yell real loudly into his ear. He always charged him ten rupees extra —early morning rates, he claimed)

2. I should have woken up well on time so I could grab the phone on the first ring—else there was a chance of my brother waking up.

Part three was **anticipated threats** which might lead to an '**Abort Mission**' and these included

1. My parents returning earlier than usual.

2. My brother picking up the telephone extension and listening in.

My calling up Vaibhav was ruled out, as I could not possibly sneak out to a telephone booth at night. During the day I had tried twice, I had to call his hostel phone. His batch mates would yell out for him. I'd hang up and call after five minutes. Both times I was told he was not in the room. I gave up after that, as it meant I had to sneak out of college between my breaks and hurry back in time for the next class. They marked attendance every hour, not just once in the morning like in school.

On my 18th birthday, I pretended to be asleep and lay still in my bed, listening to my parents leaving for their walk. The metallic clang of the latch on the gate told me they had left. I tip toed quietly into the living room where the extension of the telephone was and unplugged it. Then I went back into my parents' room and lifted the phone and listened for a dial tone. It purred contentedly. Satisfied, I placed it back. Then I double checked to see if I had placed it correctly.

When you are waiting for a phone call, time seems to really drag. If you have ever waited for a phone call you know exactly what I am talking about. You do not know what to do. You just wish and hope and will the phone to ring. You want time to fly. I sat next to the phone and waited. After a while, I slid down to the floor and continued waiting.

It rang exactly as planned and I grabbed it even before the first ring was completed.

"Hey," I managed to whisper.

Silence.

"Hello?"

Silence again.

Then I could hear the music starting. For a few seconds I had no idea what was going on. Then the penny dropped.

Craig Chaquico's Guitar solo blended perfectly with the voice of Grace Slick to make magic that day, as I listened hundreds of miles away over a phone line, at 5:45 a.m in the morning, huddled on the cold floor, the phone glued to my ear, in my parents' bedroom. It was a love song which had climbed the Bill board hot hundred charts when it had been released. At that time I could not identify the band or the artist, but later I would know that it was a song by the band Jefferson Starship. Later I would also write down the lyrics, memorize them and listen to them a hundred times over.

"Looking in your eyes I see a paradise
This world that I've found
Is too good to be true
Standing here beside you
Want so much to give you
This love in my heart that I'm feeling for you"

A guitar solo was played here. And then it continued.

The whole song took about four and a half minutes. In between, I tried telling him to stop playing the song and that I get the sentiments behind it. But he continued playing it till the very end. Then he came on the line and said

"Happy birthday Ankita and I do mean every word in the lyrics of the song".

I could have died right there and I would have been the happiest person on earth. I did not know what to say.

"Idiot," I said finally. "Why did you waste time playing the whole song? We could have talked for that much time more."

"Talk now."

"What do I say? I don't know what to say," a huge smile stretched across my face.

"You could begin by saying what a great guy I am."

"Rubbish. You are a dumbo and a fool. How did you manage it?"

"I have my ways."

Those days there were no mp3 s or CDs or I-pods for music. We listened to music on spools of tape in a cassette which we used in tape recorders. He must have hunted for the tape for this song, rewound the tape to the exact point where it started, got batteries for the tape recorder, and then carried it to the phone booth, early in the morning. It was the month of December and I knew Delhi was freezing at that time. I was amazed and touched by the effort he made.

I wanted to talk for some more time to him. I did not want the phone call to end. I was feeling elated and on top of the world. Suddenly all the crazy things that I had read in books about what people in love did were beginning to make sense. So were the countless little things that lovers in movies did.

But somewhere, sense prevailed as I also knew that if my parents came back, it would ruin a perfectly great start to a birthday, that too one which was a milestone.

"I love you, baby" He said. The way his voice went all soft and low when he said it gave me goose bumps. *He had actually said the words.*

"Hang up now," I said "And take care. Bye."

I hung up before he did. I sat on the floor and a huge smile stretched across my face.

My heart sang. I felt ecstatic. I was still smiling when I heard the metallic clang of the gate again. I ran into my room, jumped into bed, covered myself with the blanket and kept smiling, the words of "Nothing's gonna stop us now" were going round and round in my head.

Once you know what direction to take, finding the path to it becomes easy. After experiencing the super-high that 'Operation phone call' gave both of us, we wanted more of it. Compared to this, waiting for letters seemed tame. Vaibhav said he would call me every Thursday. He chose Thursday as I had been born on a Thursday. I found the gesture charming. But then, I was beginning to find anything he did for me charming.

Each Thursday there would be so much to tell him when he called. This was in addition to the letters. I wanted to share so much with him. Every minute detail had to be shared, and he was just as eager to listen. He said he loved the sound of my voice. He said he could picture me sitting on the floor in my parents' bedroom and talking to him. He always began with a "Hey" in that low baritone which I had grown to love and ended by saying "Take care, ok? I love you." His voice always went low and syrupy when he said that. I loved it.

He could have repeated that line a million times and I would have never tired of hearing it. What amazed both of us was that there was always so much to say. We never ran out of things to talk about. Each call must have lasted for about six or seven minutes as that was all he could afford and it somehow was never ever enough. I once mentioned to him that I could send him money for the phone calls as I felt guilty that he was spending so much. He wouldn't even hear of it and we never discussed it again.

On one Thursday, during yet another operation phone-call, my parents came back earlier than expected. I nearly jumped out of my skin when I heard the main entrance door of the house opening. I must have been so engrossed that I hadn't heard the giveaway metallic clang of the gate. There was no time to dash out. I panicked, hung up, rolled over and hid under the bed.

Seconds later, my dad and mom walked straight into the bedroom. My heart was pounding and I felt like a burglar. I was desperately thinking up excuses to say if they found me there. The phone rang again. Vaibhav must have presumed that the line had got disconnected. My dad answered it and hung up when there was no reply from the other end. I lay under the bed, as still as a rock. And fortunately for me, neither of my parents discovered me. I lay there for at least forty five minutes, till my dad went out of the room. My mother was in the kitchen. I could tell by the sounds.

Later I crawled out and bolted to safety, feeling exactly like a commando who moves from one trench to another, during war time. I knew Vaibhav would call the next day. And I was back at the phone, waiting.

He did.

"Idiot," I said "I nearly died. I had to lie under the bed for forty five minutes. You are a fool of the first order. Why the hell did you call back? You should have used your brains!"

He laughed and laughed some more. I laughed along with him, delighted to hear the sound of his laughter.

"How was I to know?" he said when he finally stopped laughing. "I nearly jumped out of the phone booth myself when your dad answered."

I hung up quickly that day. I did not have the stomach to risk another trench operation.

3

Election Selection

The college elections in Kerala are a huge event as they are heavily politicised. It gave a good indication of which party would form the next Government. It was well known that political parties sponsor the campaign expenses of the students' wing of their respective parties. Posters are put up all over the town, especially at the places which students frequent. There are groups moving around in jeeps with loudspeakers blaring out announcements all around the campuses. There are fliers, and election speeches. There is intense competition and the air is electric. There were also instances where candidates were stabbed and killed because of inter group rivalry. It was a messy business.

St. Agnes wanted to steer clear of all this, and so the elections in our college were completely devoid of politics. It was a bit like school election, but on a much bigger scale. There were eight major official positions the most important being the posts of Chairperson, Arts Club Secretary and General Secretary. A notice was put up announcing the election dates and inviting nominations for the posts. Anybody could nominate a student for any position. The nomination forms had to be filled up in triplicate and submitted. It had to be endorsed by two other people.

Suvi shot into the college canteen like a rocket from her hostel and said "Did you all see the notice?"

"Yeah," said Janie. "We saw it yesterday."

"And..?" prompted Suvi

"And what?" I asked.

"Guess," she said, her eyes gleaming. Her excitement was infectious. She looked charged.

"Are you contesting? Wow! That's great!" I exclaimed.

"No you, idiot, you are."

I was stunned. Then I recovered.

"What? What nonsense! How can I contest?" A second later I asked curiously, "What post?"

"We have already filled up the forms and given your name for Arts Club Secretary," she danced.

"What an idiot you are. Didn't you think of checking with me first? And who endorsed my nomination?" I spluttered, a little indignant, a lot flattered and also slightly reluctant all at the same time.

"Smitha and Hannah," she said. They were her room mates in the hostel.

"Don't worry," Suvi assured me. "We will do all the campaigning for you. It will be fun."

"Yeah, right .It is fun for you. It is me who has to stand in front of all those people and beg for votes. I can't do it."

"Weren't you the head girl in school?"

"So? That was different. *They* chose *me*. I did not have to beg for votes."

"So—*we* choose *you*" said Suvi. "Vote for...." She shouted.

And to my surprise Janie and Charu shouted "Ankita" and they caught my hand and raised it, just like a referee of a boxing match raising the hand of a winner.

Everyone in the canteen turned to look and they continued their chants. "Ankita for Arts Secy. Vote for Ankita," they continued screaming and my classmates who were in the canteen joined in.

When my initial embarrassment was gone, it was replaced by a sense of competitive spirit. My whole class got involved. Suvi appointed herself my chief campaign coordinator and managed to collect funds. I was surprised to see people actually contributing so much money. The whole hostel was behind me too. They had to be, with Suvi around! Suvi was such a whirlwind. She motivated everybody. They made posters. They made fliers and I led them like a true Indian politician. We went all around the campus. Suvi managed to hire a huge drum and between Smitha, Hannah and herself, they managed to carry it around and make a big noise. Sandhya got a bugle too and she led the 'band'. I must admit she knew how to play it well and everybody came out to the see the unique musical entourage, cheering wildly, holding placards and posters urging all to vote for their candidate—'Ankita for Arts Secy'. Initially I felt a bit silly doing it, but when I saw the frenzy that other candidates were whipping up I did not feel out of place anymore.

My opponent was a first year pre-degree student, the equivalent of a student of Class eleven. We were now in our second year of Bachelor's degree and naturally our campaign style, content and the support we gathered was so much better and more sophisticated than what they managed.

We took our breaks in the canteen, between campaign runs and speeches. We also discussed our next move, what the strong areas were, where I needed to focus and where we needed to campaign more strongly, which pockets were ours and which were not.

"Who will you vote for, for the Chairperson's post?" asked Charu.

"Undoubtedly, Sanjana Menon." I said.

Sanjana was two years our senior and in the first year of post graduation. To me she was the epitome of a 'perfect woman'. She looked gorgeous with perfectly chiselled aquiline features, light eyes that sparkled, a clear complexion, a fashionable haircut and a wonderful diction to match. She was tall, wore trendy clothes, spoke well and oozed confidence. She had even modelled for a few print advertisements and was the cover girl in a regional magazine.

All four of us ended up voting for Sanjana as chairperson.

When the results were announced, they carried me around the campus, shouting, screaming cheering. I had won by a huge margin. Sanjana had won too and Priya was the new general secretary.

I just couldn't wait to tell Vaibhav.

The Investiture ceremony of the new office bearers was a grand event attended by almost all the students and faculty. The chief guest was a popular regional film actor. There were reporters from the media and flash bulbs went pop every few seconds. A good looking movie star surrounded by eight young ladies dressed up in saris was evidently a great photo opportunity.

It was the first time in my life that I was facing a crowd of at least 3000 people. Standing on the stage there, addressing them, with the spotlight on me, it all felt very surreal. I was a little nervous and my palms were slightly cold but I managed to deliver my short, rehearsed speech without any glitches.

After the event, the eight new office bearers went out for an official dinner, along with the Principal of St. Agnes, Sister Evangeline. It was a tradition that had been followed for many years. She lost no time in telling us about our responsibilities, our official duties and how we should set an example by our behaviour. She told us about the previous office bearers and what a wonderful job they had done, confident we would do the same. Our first task was already thrust upon us—The Management School of Cochin University had their annual cultural festival '*Symphony*' coming up and our college had been invited to participate. St. Agnes had been the overall champions last year and Sr. Evangeline stressed the importance of kicking off the year with a good start.

She need not have. We were all as eager as race horses before the start of a race. We ourselves wanted to prove our worth. We were rearing to go.

There were at least 15 events ranging from fun events like face painting, ad-world, dumb charades to serious ones like western dance, short story writing, painting and elocution. The college buses would take us to the venue which was a good 45 kilometres away and would return in the evening.

"No dirty dancing girls and no short skirts either. We don't want to *tempt* the booyzzzz," called out Sanjana, stressing on 'tempt' and stretching 'boys', mimicking Sister Bertha (who headed the literature department and was involved in all the student activities) as three of us—Sanjana, Priya and I— watched the team for western dance practising.

"You mean like this?' asked Juana, as she unbuttoned her shirt, thrust out her breasts that spilled out of lacy lingerie and did a neat pelvic movement with her right hand placed just under her belly button, a bit like a bar-dancer. I gasped in shock, as the others burst out laughing. I was beginning to discover that there was indeed something liberating about an all-woman atmosphere. Here you could be yourself totally. There were no men who would ogle at you, there was no need to watch if your bra strap showed and skirts could be as short as you liked, tops could be as transparent as plastic and nobody really raised an eyebrow. It was a capsulated, insulated world and I was slowly beginning to understand it.

"Whoa! Nice! Is it Lovable or Victoria's?" Priya called out.

"Juana, that is enough. We all know your secret fantasy to star in a cabaret musical in Madrid. Now get back to practice," said Sanjana before Juana could answer Priya's question. They were obviously used to this kind of ribaldry and fun.

"Oooh! Don't get worked up, darling," drawled Juana as she buttoned up her shirt, did another seductive move, and blew a kiss at Sanjana, who rolled her eyes.

It was Juana who had choreographed the entire song. Sanjana and Suvi helped with the costumes. The dancers wore smart soldier costumes complete with all details including the caps worn by the U.S Army Corps. The song they had chosen was a old popular wartime song. The underplayed sensuality, the uniforms, the props, the well chosen piece of music and the superbly coordinated dance movements made the whole scene look like it was right out of a movie. The girls never missed a beat. They were dancing like professionals! For all her fooling around, Juana really knew her stuff and had done a great job in coaching the girls.

"Surely we'll win western dance." I told Sanjana as I watched them, mesmerised by their performance.

"Yeah, we will. Eyes of Mahaveer guys will pop out," sniggered Priya knowingly.

Mahaveer College was a co-ed college. It was an inside joke at Agnes that even the best looking girl at Mahaveers, could not match up to an average looking girl at Agnes. And funnily it was true. At cultural events like these, the guys from Mahaveers would be trying to impress the Agnes girls desperately, and strangely there would always be very few girls in any of their own teams. There would be a lot of other management institutes too taking part and they would travel from all over India to stay in Cochin for three to four days, the duration of the festival. Here too men far out- numbered the women.

It was at *Symphony* that year that Sanjana introduced me to Abhishek, Dhiren and Christy. She already knew them from previous years and had met them many times. Abhishek was the general secretary and Dhiren was the chairman of Mahaveer College students union.

"Meet Ankita, our new Arts Club secretary," said Sanjana as she introduced us. " Ankita, watch out Christy is a great quizzer, Dhiren and Abhishek are very good at public speaking."

"And I play the guitar too," smiled Abhishek.

"Hi," I smiled as my brain registered all the information. Dhiren was tall and thin, clean shaven and dressed in a formal shirt and trousers. Abhishek was much shorter. He was stout, had a roundish face that sported slight stubble, wore glasses and looked friendly and jovial. Christy was very fair, muscular, and slightly taller than Abhishek.

"So what do you do, apart from being so pretty?" asked Abhishek as he shook my hand.

"Excuse me!" I answered. "I expected a line slightly less corny than that one."

"Oh! But it's true. You *are* very pretty."

I was amused at his blatant and shameless flattery and did not know what to say.

"Catch you later guys. We have things to coordinate" said Sanjana, stepping in to rescue me.

"Where's your list?" she asked. She and I had made a detailed list with names of participants, props needed by them, timing of their events and the venue they had to be at with dates, along with the transport details, which college bus would be picking them up, from where and at what time. It needed a lot of planning and I had written it all down in a beautiful thick hard bound, brown leather diary, which was my dad's gift to me. The diary also had a lot of high quality glossy pictures of paintings by great artists. I really liked the diary and it had come in very handy. I took it out of my bag and both of us went over the details together, along with Priya and the other office bearers.

We made three teams consisting of two office bearers and decided that each team would be present at the three different venues where the events were taking place, so that if any contingency arose we could take care of it. Sanjana and I headed to the Ravi Varma auditorium where the public speaking and later the western dance events would take place. What I did not anticipate was that a contingency would arise at our venue.

"Hey Ankita. There's nobody for English Elocution from our college," said Suvi in a panic.

"What happened? Jeena was supposed to be here. What about Sindhu? How can both not be there?" I asked the panic beginning to show in my voice, as I looked at my diary. The event was about to start in 20 minutes and it was the first event of the day.

"Jeena's grandma died this morning. She got a phone call and had to go. Sindhu has laryngitis and is not able to speak even a word. I found all this out just now when the second bus came from the hostel."

"Damn! What do we do?" I looked at Sanjana in dismay.

Jeena and Sindhu were excellent orators and had won it the previous year. They were strong candidates and without them, I felt crippled.

I really admired Sanjana's calmness. "These things happen," she said unruffled. "Don't worry. I'll step in for Jeena and you for Sindhu." she said.

"What? Me?" I was aghast. "I have never done this before."

"Calm down. There is no other option. We will lose points if there is a no-show. You'll just have to step in."

I stood there in the auditorium that day, feeling foolish, ill-prepared and very small as I took the mike and spoke on the topic of the day which was "Is the Mandal Commission report justified?" I had no idea what I said. I had not read the Mandal Commission reports in the papers. Sanjana was very well informed about it. Apparently in her third year, she had just written a paper on it. I stammered and muttered and spoke for about two and a half minutes before concluding and stepping down, my cheeks burning with embarrassment and shame. Sanjana spoke beautifully and the auditorium resounded with wild cheering after she finished.

"You were not bad at all for a first timer," comforted Sanjana, later.

"Not bad? I was a disaster. I spoke for less than three minutes."

"The maximum time allowed is six minutes anyway. Three minutes is really not bad," she insisted.

When the results were announced, Abhishek had come first, Sanjana managed a second. A wild cheer went up from our girls in the audience and I joined in their cheering. I was relieved that we got at least a second place. Every point would help in the tally for overall championship which was our aim.

The second day of Symphony went off smoothly, with no absentees, no hitches and everything running like clockwork. My legs hurt from being on my feet for long hours and I realised it was a painful mistake to wear high heels. We were in the second place for overall championship by the end of the day.

In the bus on the way home, Priya said "We all saw Abhi hovering around you the whole day today, especially when you sat down. He just wouldn't leave your side."

"Come on!" I said "He chose to sit there just like that. Just to make small talk, I guess. Dhiren and Christy were sitting too. It's not like I was sitting with him exclusively. And he looks like that at everybody. You should know!" I defended myself.

"No, I do know him. Abhi is not like the rest of the guys. Now, Christy being like that would be natural. Do you know what Christy did last Valentine?"

"What? " I asked curiously.

"He gave fourteen red roses and fourteen 'I love you' cards."

"Wow, to you?" I asked.

"Well, technically the correct answer would be yes. But apart from me, he also gave it to thirteen other girls," she laughed.

Everybody joined in the laughter.

"And whom did Abhi give it to?" I asked, curiosity now getting the better of me.

"No-one!" said Priya triumphantly. "See, he was waiting for you!"

"Shut up," I said. But I smiled.

On the third day of *Symphony*, the tables turned in our favour. It was a close call. We managed to win the overall championship by just 10 points and this was because of our victory in Western dance. Our girls had danced exceedingly well.

"YEEEEEEEEEEEAAAH" yelled the girls, deafening everybody when they heard the compere announcing it. They jumped. They shouted they cheered. They fell over themselves hugging each other. Sanjana and I had already run backstage.

I hugged Juana and all the dancers.

Juana was crying with joy.

"Three cheers for St. Agnes. Hip Hip…" said Sanjana

"HURRAH" yelled the girls.

It was late in the evening by the time the prize distribution ceremony began. We felt great collecting the huge gleaming trophy for the overall championship of Symphony that year. Sanjana, Priya and I collected it and then we called all the other girls on stage. Sr. Evangeline, Sr. Bertha and all of them would be really happy. We hadn't let them down. More importantly it was a huge boost for us, as we had not let ourselves down. Our confidence in our abilities soared with this victory. It wasn't easy but we had done it.

"Winner's treat. Join me for a cup of coffee?" asked Abhishek, after the entire event was over. I had been on my feet the whole day and I was very hungry and suddenly tired. The cup of coffee was tempting, but I wasn't sure I wanted to go with Abhishek. I looked for Suvi to bail me out, but she was nowhere to be seen.

"Go on, I know you badly want that coffee," said Priya. "I'd have joined you but I'm waiting for Juana and the girls. They are changing and I am the guardian of time," she laughed as she held out her hands. They were full of watches and bracelets belonging to the girls in the western dance. "Go for God's sake. Don't think so much for a cup of coffee!" urged Priya again.

"Okay, let's go," I told Abhishek.

"Oh my God! You have actually agreed? I cannot believe my luck! I must check my horoscope for today."

"Shut up," I smiled, "I do need that coffee."

We walked to the canteen which was on a small hillock, a ten minute walk from the auditorium. He ordered cutlets too, as we sat down. I pulled up an extra chair and he ran to get it out for me.

"Come on, just tell me to get it. Ladies should never pull up chairs for themselves."

"Ladies shouldn't put up their feet either, but excuse me I'm going to do just that. Sorry." I said, as I propped my feet on the extra chair he had just pulled up.

We sat in silence, eating cutlets and having that much needed cup of coffee. I was completely immersed in my thoughts and in the events of the day. My reverie was suddenly broken when Abhi said "Hey, Aren't those your college buses, heading back?"

I looked at the two yellow buses making their way down the hill and jumped up. As the buses turned I could see the girls leaning out and yelling in chorus in a sing song voice, "Have fun. Enjoy. See you at college."

I looked at Abhi and he smiled and shrugged. I was so angry with the girls. How could they be so callous, leaving me behind and how in the world could they presume that I wanted to spend time with Abhi?! I was angry with Suvi, because I expected her to have convinced the others. Then again, a group of girls, high on adrenaline pumped by victory can be absolutely crazy and I doubted if they would have listened to her. But the immediate problem on hand was to get back to college which was a good 45 kilometres away. It was already 7.30.P.M and I could get a public bus, provided I walked to the bus stop and waited there. I didn't even know at what time the next bus would arrive, and wasn't sure if it was safe waiting in the bus stop all by myself, at this hour that too-in a deserted remote area. Most of the students stayed on campus itself and most used their own vehicles to reach the city. Nobody really used the state transport buses.

"Look," said Abhi, "I can drop you back."

"I can take a bus."

"I'll wait with you in the bus stop then. But the last bus might have already left. We'd just be wasting our time."

I still hesitated.

"Hey, I am not such a bad guy. I promise madam that you'll be safe with me."

I agreed. I didn't have much choice anyway. Later I would know that this was all a part of an intricate plan that Abhi had hatched along with Priya, Sanjana and the other girls, just so that he could get me to ride on his bike with him. Thankfully I did not know it at that point. Otherwise I'd probably have exploded with rage.

"See, I have a Bullet," He said as he wheeled out his motor bike proudly.

"The only bullet that makes an impact on me is the one you put to your head." I said.

He laughed and started the bike.

"Don't try your stupid 'braking suddenly' tricks with me, " I warned him, as I sat behind him, suddenly feeling awkward and a bit shy. "And listen, I am holding your shoulder but please don't get any ideas." I added, as I placed my right hand on his shoulder, to steady myself. I felt very self conscious as I did it but the last thing I wanted was falling off the bike, on this unasked for, unplanned and unexpected adventure.

"Come on, Ankita. I am already in heaven. And I am not that cheap too, to try the brake trick. But may I ask you how you know about it?"

Every guy knows that when a woman is on the pillion with him, the easiest way for him to get to feel her is to brake suddenly and by the impact, her body would be propelled forward and would collide with his. "I have a brother. He tells me stuff." I smiled, as Abhishek accelerated and the bike sped towards the city.

4

Girl on a Motorcycle

"So what else has your brother told you?" asked Abhi, turning around slightly so that I could hear him, over the din of his bike.

"Wouldn't you love to know?" I replied.

"What?" he asked again.

"I'm not going to elaborate and hey, please don't keep turning around to talk to me. It's making me nervous and please keep your eyes on the road."

"Yes' Ma'am," he said and he was true to his word. I was beginning to relax a little now. But at the same time I was feeling a strange kind of guilt, that I was being somewhat disloyal to Vaibhav. It was crazy, I rationalised. It wasn't as though I *wanted* to go on a bike with Abhi, and it is not even as though I had a choice. But still that little pin prick of guilt wouldn't go away. I just pushed it to the back of my mind.

"Watch out, I am slowing down and need to apply the brake" said

Abhi. He said it three more times, each time he slowed down.

I smiled as he was really making an effort to be extra careful.

"It's okay," I finally told him after he repeated it for the fourth time "Don't worry so much. I know your intentions are not dishonourable."

"Phew, thanks for trusting," he said.

The night sky looked magnificent with an explosion of a thousand stars. The moonlight was giving everything a silver glow. It was adding to the magic and I was actually beginning to enjoy the ride. We still had about thirty kilometres of the journey left. Abhi kept checking if I was comfortable. He was driving smoothly too. I was perfectly relaxed and very comfortable by now.

The highway to Cochin passed through a small village. It was desolate as all the shops were shut and the doors to the small tile roofed houses were also shut. There were brass oil lamps with a single flame burning, flickering like they were dancing, left at the doorways of most homes. The brass lamps were floor lamps, which stood either on the floor, or on a small wooden raised platform. It was a custom in Kerala that there should be a welcoming lamp at the doorway, to usher the Goddess of wealth and good fortune in. Most villages still followed it. I wished I had a camera to capture the beauty of the scene—the glow of the brass lamp and the beauty of the tiled house against the darkness of the night in the background. I took a snapshot in my head.

After the village, on the outskirts of it, there were a few push-carts selling hot *dosas* and steaming *idlis* and *appams.* It was the equivalent of *dhabhas* in Northern India. Truck drivers usually frequented these joints.

"Shall we stop?" asked Abhi "The food is really delicious here. These pushcarts are called *Thatu kadas.* Have you ever eaten in a *thatu kada?*"

"No, but I have eaten in a *dhabha.* Stop if you want to."

"Well, you don't get *dosas* and *appams* in a dhabha. You must try it. You won't regret, I promise" he said, as he stopped. We got off the bike and walked towards the *thatu kada.*

There was a wooden bench and we both sat on it as Abhi asked for a plate of *Dosa* and *Appam.* The guy at the shop was looking at us strangely. So were the few truck drivers whose trucks were parked nearby and they were eating there. Obviously a young couple on a bike, late at night, in conservative Kerala, could imply only one thing in their books.

Abhi sensed my discomfort and said "Ignore them. Just look at me and concentrate on the food."

"Are you sure this is safe?" I asked moving a little closer to him instinctively.

"Relax—you are in my land. This is *ende Keralam.* And nothing will go wrong if you're with me. " He smiled confidently.

The *Appams* and *dosas* we had were the most delicious that I had tasted so far in my life. We topped it with a cup of steaming hot tea. The feeling of a full stomach with completely satiated taste buds, a nice atmosphere and good company under a night sky is one of the most pleasant things that one can experience. I was content and I was happy. Abhi cut into this feeling almost immediately

"Hey, I have to tell you something," he said and his tone was one that I instantly recognised. It put me on high alert. I had heard the same tone in Vaibhav's voice.

God, please let him not spoil this lovely time we have had by confessing his love for me, I thought.

"Ankita, I really love you," he said.

I didn't know what to say. I looked away. Then I turned back.

I was speechless.

"You've known me for what, three days?" I said finally.

"I am not kidding, Ankita. I fell in love with you, the moment I saw you. I have never felt like this about anyone before, trust me. I am crazy about you. Honestly. And I have never done anything like this before in my life. This confessing feelings and all, is just not me, but with you I really cannot hold back anymore," he said looking straight into my eyes. His eyes shone with a sincerity and kind of desperate manic glint that was hard to comprehend.

I was completely taken aback. I did not expect a 'bare-it-all' even though I had half anticipated it when he said he had something to say. But I did not think he would be so forthright and so open about it.

There was only one thing to do. To tell him about Vaibhav.

So I did.

"I do have a boy friend."

"And who is this person, may I ask? Is it someone I know?"

"No, you don't know him. He's a classmate of mine. We went to school together. He is in Delhi now."

The relief on his face was almost instant.

"So, he is not even here."

A moment later he added, "And why don't I believe you?" he asked searchingly, looking at me with a glazed look.

"Ummm—Maybe because you cannot see him?"

"Ha ha ha" he laughed "That's because you just made him up and he does not exist!" He said triumphantly.

"Oh no, he does. I did not mean it that way," I hastily clarified.

"I'm sure you just made it up to fob me off. But I don't give up so easily."

"Look," I said "I cannot do anything to convince you. It is the truth."

"Priya told me you don't have a boy friend."

"You asked Priya about me?! What does she know about me? You should have asked Suvi. She is one of my closest friends."

"I mean what I said, Ankita. Please don't say anything. Please think about it. That's all I ask of you."

"Look, we've had a great time. Let's forget all this. You drop me back." I said as I walked towards his bike.

We completed the rest of the journey in silence.

The next day was a holiday due to some festival and I was glad as it gave me some time to rest and think about things. The shrill ring of the phone woke me up the next morning when my parents had gone for their walk. It was Suvi. She said Abhi was at the college gate a little while ago, asking for her. He had lied to the hostel warden that he was her cousin. Suvi had presumed that it had something to do with me and had met him. He had given her my brown leather diary which I had forgotten in the Auditorium. He had found the lyrics of the song "Nothing's gonna stop us" which I had scribbled on a piece of paper. He was convinced that I had written the lyrics for him and was now playing hard to get. He had said all this to Suvi and had also given her a sealed envelope which she was to deliver to me. Suvi said that he would just not believe her when she tried to tell him the truth about Vaibhav.

What an idiot Abhi was. How could he presume that I wrote the song for him. Why didn't he just believe Suvi me or?

I just couldn't wait to reach college that day. Suvi and I bunked the first class and went to the college library. The library was huge and there were many corners where we could talk undisturbed. She handed me the letter as well as my diary that Abhi had given her. It was a sealed yellow envelope with the address in small neat writing,.

"Go on," smiled Suvi "Open it," she urged, oblivious to my inner turmoil and confusion. I did not want to open the letter. I dreaded it. I felt it was wrong. I felt I was betraying Vaibhav.

"I don't feel like," I whispered.

"Don't be an idiot. Here, let me open it," she said grabbing it.

"Noooo!" I said, snatching it back from her and keeping it in my diary. I'll open it at home.

"I want to see what he has written. Open it, open it," she urged.

"Yes, you shall read it fully, but only after I am ready," I said with an air of finality as I closed the diary and stood up.

I opened it later, at home after I had bolted my door. He had used expensive handmade paper. His writing was small, precise and very neat.

Dearest Ankita, he had begun and I cringed. I was not his dearest.

Pardon my addressing you as dearest, but right now that is how I feel towards you.

I almost jumped—Good Lord, could he read my mind?!

You have given my life a new direction and nothing has mattered so much to me till now. Swami Vivekananda had said "We are what our thoughts have made us. So take care what you think. Thoughts live. They travel far." Right now Ankita, my thoughts are centred only on you. I cannot think of anything else but you. I have stayed up the whole night thinking and re-thinking and I am swept away by the depth of my own emotions. I have tried not to act like this. I hate it, but cannot help it.

God, you are lovely and really very beautiful. But that is not why I feel like this towards you. I love the way you speak, the way you smile and the way you are so easily shocked. I love the enthusiasm you have and how you think that you have to do it all. I love the way you come up with repartees and you work so hard to make things happen. I loved the way you warned me on the bike to behave myself (Trust me, even if you hadn't I would have treated you with utmost regard. You deserve of so much). I love your spirit and the way you spoke on Mandal Commission that day at Symphony, even though you knew nothing about it. I admired your courage to go up on stage. You may not have won a prize that day but in my mind you were clearly a winner.

I love the way your eyes sparkle when you speak. They seem to dance to the rhythm of your words. You are so full of zest. You inspire me and make me want to be like you. I love the way that wisp of hair falls across your forehead and the way you keep tucking it behind your ears. Oh yes—I loved your white high heels too. I loved the black top you wore and the slits that it had at the side and the way you kept tugging it down so that your skin wouldn't show. I loved the silver bangle you wore on the first day and the thick white one with little polka dots you wore on the second day. I loved the silver ear-rings and the mismatched gold chain. Yes, I noticed! I noticed every little thing about you.

I couldn't help smiling at his words. He really seemed to have noticed every minor detail about me. The first page ended here and he had written "P.T.O" at the bottom. I smiled as the last time I had used it was in school, in our assignments when I wanted the teacher to turn the page, just in case she missed it.

I was more than ready to turn over. "Oh God. Abhi writes so much better than Vaibhav." The thought crept up surreptitiously into my head and I guiltily and hastily pushed it aside and admonished myself for comparing them both. When I turned over I recoiled, nearly jumped out of my bed and hit the roof, as though I had settled down on a hot scalding iron instead of my comfortable pillows. Written in blood in letters about two inches high, in capitals were the words

"I LOVE YOU"

The first few letters were darkest and the O and U were very light. And beneath them he had written in pen, *yes, it is blood and I do love you, but I think I don't even have enough blood in my body to prove my love to you.*

On the next page at the bottom left hand side, he had stuck a photo of himself which he had cut out in shape (I presumed from a larger photo which perhaps had other people). Beneath it, he had written

I may not be a pro-Mandal Commission activist or a reservationist but I surely want to reserve you for myself.

I want to talk to you for a little while. Please don't say no. I'll be waiting.

All my love and then some more,

Abhi

And below this he had written his phone number, address and drawn a map to his house. It was a route I was familiar with, as I knew that part of the town and he had indicated all the landmarks and important places. I could make out where his home was easily. The directions were clear and well emphasised.

My heart seemed to be beating at the rate of million times a minute now. I did not know what to do. Curiously I sniffed the letter, the part which he had written in blood. It smelled like rust. I found myself wondering whether he had cut himself and if so what finger he had cut. Had he cut his thumb? Had he cut his forefinger? This guy seemed to be crazy. Yet it was a manic, intense kind of craze.

I waited for a chance to call Suvi. When my mother stepped out in the evening to visit a neighbour, I grabbed my chance and dialled her hostel number. The common phone was very close to her hostel room and she came on the line almost immediately.

"Did you read it? What has he said? Tell me, tell me!" she demanded, without even a cursory hello. We were beyond that.

"He has said he wants to meet me for just a little while," I answered, feeling weird, confused and not knowing what to do, all at the same time.

"Ah-ha! What has he written?"

"What do you think? He has also drawn a map giving directions to his home and says he will be waiting for me."

"What are you going to do?"

"Idiot, why do you think I called you?"

"Meet him," she said giggling wickedly.

"Shut up. Stop making fun of me!"

"No, I actually meant it. The guy seems obsessed. He has written to you sincerely. I think you should at least meet him and explain."

"I thought of it too. But I don't know Suvi, it seems absolutely wrong."

"Gosh Anks! Stop pretending you're married to Vaibhav. And you are not in the Victorian era. How proper and idealistic can you be? Get a hold on yourself, girl. Sometimes you're such a people pleaser, no actually that should be Vaibhav-pleaser."

"I am NOT," I defended myself. But I knew she had a point. I did tend to be idealistic and most of the time my behaviour was governed by what Vaibhav would say, how he would react and what he would think.

"You don't have to say anything to Vaibhav. You're only meeting Abhi, not sleeping with him for God's sake. At least I presume you won't, the first time," she teased.

"Shut up!" I smiled. "See you tomorrow at college."

"Yeah, bye and don't forget to bring the letter," she reminded me before hanging up.

I thought about what Suvi said. I owed Abhi an explanation. I had to make him understand how I felt about Vaibhav. I had to tell him that I did mean what I had told him earlier. At least that is what I convinced myself.

I looked at my watch quickly. Mum would not be back for at least half an hour. I dialled his number. He answered even before the first ring had ended. It looked as though he had been waiting for it.

"Hello, Abhi?" I asked hesitatingly.

"I knew you would call!" he exclaimed triumphantly. "When are you coming?"

"Did I tell you I would be coming?" I retorted, a little shocked at how well he seemed to have gauged me.

"Of course you will!" he answered with certainty. "Tell me when, what time?"

"Ummm, let me think about it. If you're really nice and plead with me I might consider it," I smiled, enjoying prolonging his eagerness and anticipation.

"Oh, I can beg, I can play the violin, I can bring loudspeakers outside your house right now or flowers if you prefer."

I was sure he was capable of it.

"No need for all that, I'll meet you on Saturday afternoon at 3?"

"Waiting, waiting, waiting" he said and then we said polite byes and hung up.

When Vaibhav called I did not mention a word about Abhi or agreeing to meet him even though it was topmost on my mind at that point of time. If guilt was a stone tied to my ankles, I would have sunk easily to the bottom of the sea. But I wore it easily on my sleeve, by pushing it aside and spoke to Vaibhav as though everything was normal.

When I reached college the next day, Suvi pounced on me, grabbed my bag, rummaged expertly through the contents and found the letter.

"You would make a good thief. You go through the contents of my bag so quickly and deftly," I commented watching her.

"Only if all the bags had interesting love letters," she retorted, as she began reading.

She too reacted exactly as I had when I had first read it and I waited, watching for the effect when she would turn the page and see the writing in blood. I had purposely not mentioned it over the phone. I wanted to see her reaction, in person. She did not disappoint.

"Holy Cow, Sweet Jesus, Holy Spirit and Mother Mary!" she exclaimed.

Then when she recovered I asked her if she thought Abhi was crazy or a bit unbalanced after reading the letter.

"He is not a lunatic or unbalanced, but he is so madly in love with you. You're blind not to be able to see it."

I took a long time on Saturday morning deciding what to wear. I had already told my mother that I had a special office bearers meeting. It was really not a lie as I was meeting another office bearer, wasn't I? I chuckled at my own silly joke, but it was mostly to hide the nervousness I felt. I knew Abhi would notice what I wore. I didn't want it to seem like I had made a huge effort in dressing up to look pretty just for him. Yet, I wanted to look nice. Finally, after very long I ended up wearing a white shirt, jeans and casual brown sandals tying up my hair in a pony tail, taking care to make it seem as though no effort had gone into choosing the outfit or hairstyle or accessories.

Then (finally) when I was satisfied, I left for Abhi's house.

5

Life is what you make it

Abhi's back was turned to me and he seemed to be watching cricket on television eagerly when I arrived. I had caught a glimpse of him through the window which had a curtain that was drawn back. I was nervous and excited and suddenly unsure of myself. What was I doing, turning up at his house just because he had asked me to? After all I hadn't even known him for long. How could I get carried away like this, just because he had written me a nice letter? For a moment I considered turning back and going home. I could always call him and say that something had turned up and I couldn't come, he would never know. But then I rang the bell.

Abhi jumped up almost immediately and switched off the TV. He saw me through the window and his face broke into a wide grin.

"Welcome, welcome," he boomed as he opened the door and held out his hand.

"Hi," I smiled as we shook hands, as though we were meeting formally for a business meeting. He led me to the drawing room which was tastefully done up and motioned to me to sit down. I sank into a plush coffee brown three seater sofa and he took a seat on the arm chair, beside me. The whole place had an understated elegance. The stream of light flowing in through the window made the atmosphere very cheerful. I forgot my initial hesitation and immediately felt at home.

"God, I was waiting and waiting. I was so scared you had changed your mind," he said.

"I am on time. I had mentioned three, hadn't I?" I replied.

"Oh yes, but when you are waiting for something important, every minute seems an hour. I am so glad you came."

I knew only too well, having waited the same way for Vaibhav's phone calls. But I said nothing and smiled.

An elderly looking gentleman emerged from another room, which I presumed was the kitchen. He was tall, with a mop of gray hair, looked distinguished and wore a white Kurta and a dhoti.

"*Appacha*, this is Ankita, my friend from college," said Abhi, introducing me.

"And Ankita, this is my darling grandfather," he said.

I immediately stood up, out of respect. Years of schooling in a system which drilled Indian values in you, like respect for the elderly, was hard to do away with.

"Hello Sir," I said automatically.

"Hello young lady! And there is no need to stand! Do have a seat." he greeted me, his eyes twinkling. He sounded warm and friendly. I could sense the camaraderie between Abhi and his grandpa almost instantly.

"Are you in the same college?" he asked

"Oh no, I am from St. Agnes."

"Oh, so you're now hobnobbing with the enemy, eh Abhi?" he joked.

"Enemies only at cultural festivals. Friends beyond those," Abhi smiled.

"Anyway, Mahaveers can never beat St. Agnes. That is for sure," I boasted emboldened by his grandfather's friendliness.

"Ha ha ha. Oh yes, I have to agree with you there. Agnes girls are very smart indeed," said Abhi's grandpa.

"We will wait and see. Youth fest is not yet over," said Abhi, pretending to be offended, but I could see that he was feeling very pleased that his grandfather seemed to approve of me.

"I want to watch the cricket match. Why don't you both go upstairs?" said his grandfather as he switched on the television.

Abhi looked at me questioningly to ask if that was okay. I shrugged.

"Okay, let us go upstairs," I said and followed Abhi as he led the way up.

Following him to his room is really not a good idea, my inner voice was beginning to tell me. But like before, I shut it up, acted nonchalant and followed him. I realised I was leaving a 'safe zone'. The bedroom was positively dangerous territory. My inner voice was grumbling and shaking a disapproving finger at me now. But I was on a high. I was doing something that I had never done before. I was also curious to see what his room looked like. Besides, I had already agreed to come to his home and it was his grandfather who had suggested we go to his room, not him or me. How could I back out now?

"Wow!" I said as I entered. I couldn't help it. The room looked like it had been plucked right out of the pages of an interior design magazine and planted there. It was quintessentially male. There was a single bed, neatly made, with a masculine geometric striped, blue duvet, soft fluffy pillows with matching striped pillow cases and a chest of drawers beside it. There was a bookshelf on the wall with books neatly arranged. The chest of drawers had a framed photo of a very beautiful lady. There was a large comfortable leather arm chair which faced the bed at a forty five degree angle. There was a cosy rug and a reading lamp beside the bed. There was a basketball and a football in a little open wooden box in the corner. There was also a guitar neatly propped up against the wall. The windows had bamboo blinds. The moment you entered the room, a feeling of warmth enveloped you and you had to fight the urge to curl up on the cosy arm chair with a book.

"Your room is so neat!" I exclaimed.

"I like some kind of order and I try to keep it neat," he said. He looked pleased.

"Me too! My room is also very tidy and I would love it if you could see it." I said, feeling a bit surprised at myself. Why was I angling for his approval?

"Show me! I'd love to see it," he grabbed the hint.

"No way! My parents would never agree to a guy coming home."

"Oh Ankita! You can be such a kid! Your parents don't have to know about everything!" he winked.

I felt a blush creeping up my face and tried my best to hide it. "What are you suggesting Abhi?" I asked, looking at him straight in the eye.

"To see your room of course!" He answered without missing a

beat, looking right back, into my eyes without wavering. "Why? What did you have in mind?" His eyes twinkled.

I couldn't believe it. His voice had a very suggestive tone now. And to my horror, I found I liked it. I looked away, trying to hide my confusion.

"My room of course, I don't know what you had in mind though." I answered smiling, as soon as I recovered from my confusion.

I sat in the arm chair and leaned back, drawing my feet under me, tucking them in and settling down comfortably.

"So tell me, won't you ever even consider showing me your room?" he asked as he perched on the bed and placed a pillow in his lap, leaning forward and resting his arms on the pillow.

"Let me think about it," I smiled, enjoying this now. Abhi had dazzled me completely with his charm and audacity. I seemed to have forgotten about Vaibhav. My inner voice squeaked again trying to remind me to tell him about Vaibhav. But somehow at that moment, Vaibhav and everything to do with him seemed so far away. I was having such a good time that I didn't want anything to spoil it.

"Aren't you scared? Coming to a single guy's room like this?" He asked. He was teasing me now.

"Of course not. I spent almost half the night with you, on your bike, remember? Or have you forgotten already? " I retorted.

"Ha Ha Ha," he guffawed. "That I agree Ankita and thank you for trusting me. I did mean what I wrote in the letter you know."

"I must tell you that the blood bit freaked me out completely. Did you actually cut your hand? Which finger?" I asked curiously.

"See," he said as he held up his hand. There was a cut on the ring finger. Then he clutched it with his middle finger and thumb, like a pen and demonstrated in the air. "It is the first time I am doing something so desperate, Ankita. I wanted you to believe me so badly. I don't go around expressing my love to every girl I meet. I wanted you to see how sincere I was and how desperate. Gosh, you have no idea how much I love you." His eyes were shining with hope, love and sincerity. It was hard not to be swept away by him.

Looking at his face and listening to his words, I wanted to take his hand in mine and kiss his finger. I wanted to tell him that he was a great guy and I really enjoyed his company. I wanted to say that I felt honoured that he was doing all this for me. But no words came and I sat still, like a statue, not knowing what to say.

He mistook my silence for disapproval. "Look Ankita, I am really sorry to be so open. I swear I have wished a hundred times I could stop this madness of mine. But I am helpless." He gestured waving his hands in the air. "God, morning, evening and night, day in and day out all I can think about is you. Do you even realise the significance of what I am saying?"

I could not keep quiet any longer. I got up and sat next to him on the bed. "Oh Abhi, I do." I said. "I am not blind. I can see. But all this is so sudden for me. I think you're a great guy. I do enjoy your company. But..."

"Say no more," he interrupted me. "There are no buts and no ifs in life. Life is what you make it, Ankita. I am willing to wait for you forever. That is how much I care."

"Thanks Abhi."

"For what?'

"For understanding. Now end of topic. Do you want to talk about anything else?"

There was a knock on the door before he could answer. It was a lady who seemed to be the maid holding a tray with two steaming mugs of tea, some fried onion *bhajis* and ginger biscuits."

"Thank you Thresi *chechi*," he said as she kept the tray on the chest of drawers, giggled and left the room. I suddenly realised that she must have giggled because Abhi and I were now sitting on the bed, side by side, our shoulders almost touching each other.

"She must have thought we were doing something else," Abhi smiled, the mischief coming back to his voice again.

"As though we will do anything with the door open."

"Let me shut it then," he teased.

"Not so soon," I replied smiling.

"By the way Abhi, where are your parents? Do they both work?"

"My mum is no more. That's her picture you see over there," he said pointing to the lady's photo that I had earlier seen on the chest of drawers. There is so much more I want to tell you," he said. "No actually I want to show you."

"Do say. I am all ears," I said propping a pillow against the wall and leaning back on his bed. It felt so intimate to be sitting with him, like this. on his bed.

He turned around so that his back was towards me and lifted up his T-shirt. I was stupefied. It was a profusion of angry welts and bruises, some red and some fading ones, criss-crossing each other all over his back.

"God, what is it?" I said as he lowered his T-shirt and turned towards me, settling next to me, leaning against the wall. His shoulder was definitely touching mine now but I made no efforts to move away.

"That is my father." He said simply. "I hate him. I would kill him if I could."

The vehemence and determination in his voice shocked me. His openness in showing it to me also took me by complete surprise. I was feeling a plethora of emotions that I had no name to. I wanted to know more.

"He uses a belt, the bastard, pardon my language." He said simply.

"But why? What have you done to merit this?"

"It's a long story, but let me try and make it short."

"No, tell me the whole thing. I want to know."

"He does not live here. He lives in Pretoria, South Africa. He works for a missionary organisation trying to promote God's cause" he said. The derision and scorn in his voice was obvious. "And what I showed you was his reward this time to me, for my refusal to toe his line. He visits me from time to time. He wants me to join him in his mission. I hate it when he comes here. "

"Doesn't your grandpa stop him?"

"This is my mother's dad. So he has no say in the matter. My father does not even know who his parents are. He was raised by these missionaries. He will lay down his life for them and he just cannot accept the fact that I have a different view point. "

"And how did your viewpoint become so different?" I asked a wave of curiosity and affection flooding through me. I wanted to know more. I wanted to know all about this guy who was so madly in love with me.

"My mum was a Hindu. That is why it means such a lot to him if I join him. It is a kind of redemption for his having married her."

I did not know what to say. I felt like hugging him and telling him that it would all work out in the end. But who knew what the future held and the assurance sounded hollow to me.

I took his hand in mine, the one that had the cut and held it. It seemed the right thing to do at that point of time. He squeezed my hand as if he was getting some strength to go on.

We sat quietly for a long time hands entwined, shoulder to shoulder. There was so much going on inside my head. I felt strangely connected to Abhi. He made no attempt to move or to remove his hand. Finally, when it began getting dark, I said that I must go home otherwise my parents might get worried.

Something in me changed that day, with the visit. I wasn't sure what it was. There were no words to describe it. I wanted to tell it all to Suvi.

But not right away. I needed time to clear my own thoughts which were still whirling inside my head, as I fell asleep that night. It was the first time in ages that someone other than Vaibhav had dominated my thoughts.

6

The needle swings

Suvi could not wait to hear all about my visit to Abhi's place. She dragged me off to a secluded spot in the building that housed the college auditorium.

"You little minx. You slept with him. You lost your virginity! Didn't you? " she shrieked.

"Of course not! We only held hands," my indignant words were out even before I realised it.

"Ah ha! AH HA! Miss Ankita Sharma . If anybody can get you to open up and trap you to admit facts it is only me!" She looked as though she had won a prize at a fair where you try your chances in a game of luck.

I asked her to shut up and narrated in detail every single thing that had happened, ever since I went to his home.

She let out a whistle when I completed. Then she said "You should have at least kissed him."

"You and your dumb ideas! You're a trollop and that is all you can think of."

I was annoyed with her for not offering a salve to my guilt. She was only looking at it as an opportunity to get physical with a guy. A perfect opportunity that had been handed to me on a platter, which in her books, I had missed. I walked off angrily and she trailed behind me.

"Hey, relax. I was only teasing you," she said. "But look at you. You're behaving as though you actually slept with him."

"Look, I am beginning to like him a lot more than I intended to. I have no idea what to do. And what do I tell Vaibhav?" I asked.

"How do you know your sweet Vaibhav hasn't met someone there? You think he is telling you everything? For God's sake Ankita, it is not as though you are married to Vaibhav. Things happen. People change. Before I met Ravi, I liked Suresh. And all this virginity business is really no big deal. You do it and it's done."

I knew she had a sex life but this was the first time she was talking about it.

"Weren't you scared the first time? " I asked her. I wished I could be as nonchalant as her. I wished things didn't bother me so much.

"Well, not exactly scared, because I knew what I was doing. I was more worried about whether he had put on the condom right. And I was more worried about getting pregnant."

"And how did you know that Suresh was the one?" I asked.

"My sweet, Anks, which century are you living in? Don't tell me you are saving your virginity to gift it on a platter to the guy you will marry," she said.

I was.

So I said nothing. I think she understood.

"Look," she said, "I had decided to do it and I did it. That was all. It did not matter with whom. But things didn't work out with Suresh. Then Ravi came along. And even now it is not as if Ravi and I are a couple. I do understand what you're feeling, babe, trust me I have been there. I *know.*"

I felt a lot better after her assurance. I was a little in awe of her too. I had miles to go in *that* department. Here I was, feeling guilty for having spent time alone with a guy. It wasn't as if we had kissed or even got physical. But somehow I knew at that moment, that a barrier between him and me had been broken and I would go further the next time. I wasn't comfortable thinking about it, so I dealt with it in the manner I knew best. I pushed it aside.

As months passed, I discovered that being an office bearer meant a mad whirl wind of selections, competitions, trials, organising transport and the best part of it all—bringing home the laurels. For most of the cultural festivals, we either came second in the overall championship or were winners.

For each of these cultural festivals, the team from Mahaveer's would invariably be present. That meant that Abhi was there and my interaction with him grew more and more. It became almost a ritual that after each cultural festival he would ask me if he could drop me back home, after a cup of coffee. I looked forward to it. I enjoyed his company and over numerous cups of coffees and bike rides home, we were forging a bond that was becoming stronger as the weeks passed.

I did not breathe a word of any of this to Vaibhav. But deep down, I knew I wasn't waiting for his calls or letters anymore with the same eagerness that I used to.

These days I was only looking forward to opportunities that would give me a chance to be with Abhi for longer periods of time. The needle had swung in Abhi's favour and there was no question of turning back.

7

Destiny changes in moments

It was during the mother of all cultural festivals, the Mahatma Gandhi University Youth Festival, that Abhi and I first kissed. The Earth didn't move, the skies didn't open, I didn't feel the exhilaration I was supposed to feel, as described in books and shown in movies, but the cops came. The feeling of terror that swept over me when we heard the noise and saw the hurried footsteps and cops spilling out of jeeps like marbles tumbling out of an open bag, would remain with me for years to come, whenever I set my eyes on a person in a uniform.

The sequence of events that led to this, started innocently enough. At least it was innocent on my part and Abhi's but I am not so sure about the others who were involved.

It was an event spread over four days and we were all staying at a hostel in the college that was hosting it that year. The students who took part were of varied age groups ranging from 16-24. For many students, it was the first time they were staying away from home.

The freedom and the fun that this opportunity gave them, gave them a high and sometimes, as office bearers, we had to be strict with the girls.

Only the office bearers in our college had permission to stay out as late as they pleased, as there were a million things to co-ordinate for next day. Anyone else who wanted to stay out late had to get an okay from them. Three days of events were already over. It was clear that Agnes was in the lead for the over-all championship and a talented girl called Suja from our college, had already emerged as the Individual champion, as she had won the first prize in four events—two dances and two singing events. It was a well known fact that the girl who won it would be invariably be offered a role in a Malayalam movie. We were waiting to see if Suja would take it up or pass it on. We were all proud of her. She was our star, our prized possession, the darling of the nuns who taught at the college.

Suja came to me, asking if she could stay out a bit longer that night as a guy from Mahaveers who was her boyfriend had asked her out. I had no idea how to answer her. I passed the buck and asked her to talk to Sanjana.

Sometimes decisions that are taken in the nick of a moment are the ones that have the power to affect a whole train of events that follow. But at the moment of taking those decisions, not much thought goes into them. They are taken in the normal manner and in retrospect, cause a great deal of contrition or remorse.

"Do you want to join us? We're having a special office bearers party tonight," said Sanjana when Suja asked her for permission to stay out late. It was a surprise to me as well.

"What office bearers party?" I asked.

"The office bearers of all colleges are meeting today at 11.00 p.m after the day's events are over. It is a tradition before the last day, during youth festivals. Suja can come along and vanish in a little time after the party starts. Nobody need know, as long as she comes back safely and joins us to go back to the dorm," Sanjana winked.

I shrugged. It was not my decision. I was quite sure that Sanjana knew what she was doing. Of course Suja agreed gratefully. Every other office bearer seemed to know of the party. They were old hands at this and I was the newbie.

"Where is this party going to be held?" I asked Priya, as I watched Suja walk away in glee.

"At Hotel Crown Plaza. Their ballroom is a decent size. And some navy cadets will be there too. Gosh, those guys *are* gorgeous," answered Priya dreamily.

The Indian Navy had a sea officers training establishment as well as a Naval Base in Cochin. The naval cadets trained here. The guys were usually well turned out, articulate, smart and most importantly would be officers at the end of their courses. The combination was irresistible to most women and having a naval academy guy as a boyfriend was a matter of prestige. The naval guys on their part would definitely give a right arm to say that an Agnes girl was their girlfriend. After all, Agnes girls had the reputation of being intelligent, fashionable and smart. So it was a kind of symbiotic relationship and each side thought they were the lucky ones.

The girls were all excited about the party. The numerous preparations that involved 'getting ready for a party' in a woman's parlance had begun in the hostel at 6.00 p.m itself. I was stunned when I saw some of the outfits that the girls had chosen to wear. Sanjana looked like a fashion model straight out of Vogue with an off shoulder deep red dress that had a plunging neckline and it clung to every curve. She also wore six inch heels and when she completed her make-up, all our jaws dropped open in amazement. She was stunning. Most of the others who were attending the party had dressed glamorously. I had not known about the party and had not carried any such party wear with me. I chose to wear a simple black and white printed shirt and black tights. They went well with my white heels. Sanjana took me aside and asked if I would like to borrow one of her outfits but I refused.

All the girls wore some kind of a jacket or a full sleeved top over their clothes which they would remove as soon as we were out of sight of the faculty. If the nuns saw the girls dressed like this, they would definitely object.

The hotel was within walking distance of where we stayed. The party had already started when we arrived.

The atmosphere was electric. The ball room was spacious, elegant and filled with young people dancing to the groove of blaring western foot tapping numbers. I was taken by surprise and it seemed as if I had stepped into a different world.

Priya, Sanjana and the others seemed to fit right in. They mingled around effortlessly and started dancing with a group of guys. I knew they were the navy guys. Suja too seemed to have found her boy friend and they were dancing like they had eyes only for each other. I did not know what to do. I tried to blend into the background inconspicuously, suddenly feeling out of place and uncomfortable.

"Hi there. You're Ankita, aren't you?" said a tall well dressed guy, tapping me on my shoulder. From his hair cut I knew that he was one of the Naval guys.

"Yes. And how do you know me?" I answered, surprised.

"Sorry, I didn't introduce myself. I am Pravin Singh. I am a friend of Rakesh Duggal who is Suja's friend," he said.

"Yes, I have heard Suja talking of Rakesh."

I hoped that he would not ask me to dance. I was not ready to dance yet.

"May I have the pleasure of dancing with you?"

"Er...Maybe after a while?"

I did not know what the etiquette in turning down a guy was. I was beginning to sweat a little now.

"Hey Ankita! Comfy?" said a familiar voice and I saw Abhi with a drink in his hand, walking towards me.

The relief I felt was what an animal trapped in a net experiences when it is freed.

"Hey, Hi!" I said sounding so enthusiastic that I hoped Pravin got the message. He seemed to have, as he slipped away unobtrusively as Abhi came up to me.

"I am so glad to see you," I said.

"You're looking terrific! I love it when you leave your hair open." he said his eyes shining.

"I feel such a plain Jane. Look at the others."

"They need all those embellishments because they don't have what you do," he said smiling.

"And what is it I have which they don't?" I asked eagerly lapping up his praise.

"Me, of course!" he said.

I laughed and punched him playfully.

Then I peeped into his glass. "What are you having?"

"Champagne. Can I get you some?"

"No, thank you. You know I don't drink."

"I promise I am not trying to get you drunk," his eyes twinkled. "But you must try everything at least once."

I was tempted. I had never had alcohol before. I knew I could count on Abhi to see that I did not do anything foolish. I trusted him completely now. I also felt a lot braver than before, now that he was at my side. I looked around the room. Almost everyone had a drink.

"Here, try mine. See if you like it."

Hesitatingly I took a sip from his glass. It felt strangely intimate. I nodded my approval and he got me a drink.

"Have it slowly. Don't gulp it down."

"I am not so foolish. I know that much!"

The party was in full swing now. The lights had dimmed. Many of the guys were smoking and the air was thick with smoke. The smell of expensive perfumes too lingered. There was a huge disco light in the centre. The music had changed to slow dance and many of the couples were dancing very close to each other. A few of the girls had buried their faces in the guys' shoulders. They were completely engrossed in themselves. My eyes almost popped out when I saw where the hands of some guys were. I felt a bit like an intruder. Abhi too seemed to have sensed my surprise.

"This is not really uncommon, Anks," he said. "Many of them go the whole hog too. They have rented rooms upstairs."

"What?!!" I said, truly shocked now.

"Hey, look. I didn't do it! And I am not making an indecent proposition to you. Don't worry!" He said.

I was beginning to feel a bit claustrophobic. Also the alcohol seemed to have unsettled my stomach. I felt giddy.

"Abhi, I need to sit down. I am not feeling too good."

"Come, let us get out. The fresh air will do you good."

Deciding to go out at that instant was one of the best decisions I have ever made in my life. In retrospect, I would be many times grateful for it. They say destiny changes in moments sometimes.

But I did not have these philosophical thoughts at all, as I went out with Abhi into the cool night, through a door that led outside to the huge hotel lawns and the well done up garden. Abhi gestured towards a wooden bench that was tucked away, almost hidden by two large green bushes that seemed to be ushering it. The sky was star studded and the breeze felt refreshing compared to the noise, smoke and music inside.

"This is so much better," I said.

Abhi put his arm around me and I did not protest. I leaned my head on his shoulder. He stroked my hair and murmured something about how beautiful I was. I snuggled a bit closer. That was when he pulled me towards him, put an arm around my waist and kissed me so tenderly that I thought my heart would break as his lips met mine. I could taste the champagne on his lips. It felt so natural and so right. I had always wondered how my first kiss would be, what one should do—should one open the mouth, close one's eyes? Would I know what to do? I was surprised that it just came instinctively and Abhi seemed to know what he was doing. My heart was singing and more than exhilaration, it was a feeling of completeness that washed over me, in a strange way.

That was when we heard a commotion, the sudden noises and

confusion. It was the cops. We could see them tumbling out of their vehicles and running into the hotel. The scene frightened me.

We didn't know what to do. We had no idea what was happening. I wanted to go and see, but Abhi pulled me back.

"Let us wait here Ankita, Trust me, it won't be a pretty scene."

"How can I, Abhi?! We can't just sit here."

"Yes, we can. I think I know what is happening out ther e. Look, there is nothing you and I can do. You can't reason with cops. Let us stay here. Now listen to me and don't protest."

I did listen to him. We stayed on that bench for almost two hours till the noise and confusion died down.

Destiny had indeed changed in a matter of moments. The next day was a nightmare for everyone in Agnes and everyone associated with Agnes. Splashed in huge blazing headlines across the pages of almost all Malayalam dailies and a few English newspapers too were screaming headlines that said "Agnes girls caught in hotel rooms,", "Agnites show a talent of a different kind," and many more such sarcastic one liners. It was mudslinging at its worst.

We had been the celebrities of the moment and now had fallen. The rival colleges were pouncing upon it like vultures. The mighty Agnes girls were shamed. We would later find out that it was one of the office bearers of the host college who had connections with the student wings of the political parties, who had engineered this whole police drama. We would also later find out that the naval cadets who were involved had punitive action taken against them too.

Sanjana and Suja's photos were splashed across the newspapers with unpleasant and unnecessary details and also the names of the naval guys they were with. In a place like Kerala, it was a fate worse than death. The fact was that they were all over eighteen and what they were doing was entirely their business was forgotten. But conservative Kerala had no place or tolerance for such things. Good girls simply did not go to hotel rooms with men and get caught in police raids. Only prostitutes did that.

What hurt me most and disillusioned me completely was the reaction of the college authorities. They promptly expelled Sanjana and Suja. Sister Evangeline released a press statement saying how just two girls had tarnished the reputation of the college. The college had a history of more than a hundred years and never in its history had such a thing happened. They blamed the girls and their parents. Then after a hurried conference and closed door meeting with other faculty members, they announced that they were reinstating a new chairperson for the college whom they had unanimously agreed upon. Their choice of chairperson was someone the rest of us would grow to hate—she was a spineless coward who could only suck up to authority. She had no opinion of her own. She would never even have been nominated, let alone won the election, had she contested for a million years. She was plain, unglamorous, had no clue what to do and did not even know how to speak. She was a stooge not a leader.

Priya, I and all the other office bearers went and met Sr. Evangeline privately. We voiced how strongly we felt about it and that we were representing the thousands of voices of students of the college who wanted to say the same thing. Sister brushed our protests aside.

"We gave you freedom and you misused it. These girls have brought disgrace to the college. You girls have no choice but to obey," she said.

I could not help thinking that as long as the girls kept winning and bringing the laurels home, they were adored. As long as they were 'useful' and they 'performed', it was great. But the moment things went a little awry, they were dropped like hot potatoes.

Later I told Suvi bitterly "How then is the treatment meted out to these girls different from the treatment that is meted out to prostitutes? Both are used."

"You're perfectly right," she said. "At least they get paid for it."

The rest of the year was not the same. Without Sanjana to lead the team of office bearers, the entire essence of what it was all about had disintegrated.

The college authorities did not care. Agnes had already won almost every cultural competition that there was to win that year. Agnes was also the overall champion in the Mahatma Gandhi University festival that year.

But it was the first time that nobody talked about it or rejoiced.

8

Ready to fly

The elections arrived like monsoons the next year. It was the final year of our graduation and we would soon be completing our Bachelor's degrees. There was no way I was contesting. I had made up my mind about that even though many had urged me to contest again. The entire thing had left a sour taste in my mouth.

There were only a few more months for our final year to end. My agenda was now to get into any of the top institutes in the country offering an MBA. Like many of the others, I had dutifully filled in the application forms, taken out the demand drafts and mailed them well before the last dates. My parents were very happy about my decision. I hoped I would not disappoint them. I desperately wanted to get admission into an MBA course.

Vaibhav and I were still in touch but not with the intensity as earlier. I think it was more out of a sense of duty that he called rather than anything else. I had not even noticed that his calls had trickled as I was so absorbed in Abhi and the other things that were going on in my life. I think the love I had for him was replaced by a kind of fond affection. Honestly it did not matter to me anymore whether he called or not. It seemed as though Abhi and I had been through so much together and somewhere along the way, Vaibhav had been left far behind.

Charu had decided that she would pursue Chartered Accountancy and join her father's firm. The rest of us had no such options and the entrance tests were what we had to concentrate on. The MBA bug had bitten all of us. Most of us had opted for postal coaching. There were only two reputed institutes that sent you the practice papers and the study material. We pooled in our resources. We had formed a study group which consisted of Dhiren, Abhi and Christy from Mahaveers and Suvi and I from our college. We met twice a week at Mahaveers, in their auditorium which we had access to, as Abhi and Dhiren were office bearers again that year.

Christy and I were the ones who were most serious about it. We competed with each other like crazy, solving questions, seeing who would crack it first. I was far ahead of him in verbal ability and he would be dazzled by my reading speed and data interpretation. But he made up for it in quantitative ability. He beat me hollow in that, as I grappled with figures. I knew how to solve most of it, but my speed wasn't very good. I took too much time. On some days, we had seniors over, from our college and from Mahaveers, who were now doing an MBA at Cochin University of Science and Technology (CUSAT).They joined us and they gave us tips. They held mock-interviews and group discussions as well. I kept telling Abhi that he would have to work harder. I felt that the college activities were taking a toll on his preparations. I sensed that he did not like my saying so and could also see that he was getting annoyed at the way I competed with Christy. But my goal was clear and I was not wavering from it. I was determined to make it.

I think entrance exams are mostly about how one performs on that particular day. Of course, it needs hard work and talent, but largely it also needs luck.

Whatever it was, I was delighted beyond measure when I got an interview call from not one, but four institutes one of which was a well known one in Bombay! I had also been selected for CUSAT. I had never expected to be this lucky. I cleared the group discussion and interviews too. My parents' joy knew no bounds, as they boasted to all relatives about my achievement.

Abhi had got an interview call only from CUSAT.

My dad had another surprise for me. He announced that he had got a promotion in his company and had been posted to Bombay. We would soon be relocating as soon as my final exams were over. Abhi was very upset when he heard this.

"Look Abhi," I reasoned with him, "Even if my folks were not moving to Bombay, we would still have parted as I would have chosen to do it in Bombay," I said.

"Come on Anks, Isn't CUSAT good enough for you? Doesn't 'WE' mean anything to you?"

Most of us had got offer letters from CUSAT and those who had got interview calls from other places were stalling, keeping CUSAT as a backup option, in case we did not get in anywhere else. CUSAT was definitely not my first choice.

"Abhi, how can you be so unreasonable?" I said. "Look, put yourself in my place. If *you* had got a call from the places I have, wouldn't you have grabbed it?"

"No, Ankita. I would still have gone to the place where both of us can study together. That is how much you mean to me," he said simply. I did not know what to answer as I knew he meant it too. But the thing was, he had not made it. I had.

He was such an emotional fool. This was an opportunity of a lifetime for me. How could I just chuck it up, for something which I presumed was love? How foolish was that? I was not getting swayed. Abhi felt I was being hard hearted. I felt I was being practical and rational.

"Look, I had told you to study hard. If you had, you would have made it," I said. It came out more accusingly than I intended.

"Yes. It is easy for you to say now, Miss. Bombay. You know what, pride has gone to your head." he said caustically.

I was taken aback. I said no more and walked away.

"Don't get angry with me," he called out. "I am the only one who dares to tell you the truth. The others just suck up to you. Think about it."

I was fuming. How dare he speak to me like that? He called out to me to wait, but I was in no mood to listen to him.

Later I thought about what Abhi had said. I concluded he was frustrated and jealous as he had not made it. How could he ask me to give up my dream? How could he ask me to give up something I had worked so hard for, just so I could be with him? CUSAT did not look appealing at all. In the dazzle and glamour of Bombay, what chances did it have? I did not feel any regret about leaving my friends behind.

Bombay beckoned and I was more than ready to fly.

9

Never Belittle Love

There was still a month left before we would finally move to Bombay. Everything seemed to have worked out perfectly for me. Like the pieces of a jigsaw puzzle, my life was falling into perfect order and was coming together in a way I never imagined. My parents felt that my dad's transfer to Bombay was the next best thing to have happened, after my getting into one of the finest MBA programmes that was on offer. They were also delighted that my brother had got into John Hopkins University in the USA and he would leave soon.

Most days I went out to meet the gang and now my parents did not even question me when I said that I was going out. It was like I had earned the right to do what I pleased. Almost everybody from our gang of friends would be starting their courses in the next two months. For all those who were doing courses outside Kerala, these were the last few weeks in Cochin, which had been home to us, for the last three years. We felt a tinge of sadness we would be leaving it, even though the future seemed very bright.

All of us wanted to make the most of the last few days left and our favourite haunt was a restaurant called '*Appu aur Pappu*' which faced the backwaters. Despite its ridiculous name which we had shortened to Appu's, the ambience was great as it had outdoor seating around two large shady trees, facing the promenade. The salty sea breeze blowing gently around us seemed to knit us together as we sat nursing our mocktails and munching snacks that we ordered as we watched people walking on the promenade. The sunset made the sea sparkle with a million shades of orange and gold and we hung around, our faces glowing in the mellow light, talking, laughing, joking until it grew dark and we could see no more. Then we decided that it was time to go home.

Abhi was there on all days. I had not met Abhi separately since the time I had angrily walked away from him, refusing to hear his apologies. I always made sure to meet him only as a part of the gang. I did not even want to hear what he had to say. So I always arrived a little later than the others and left a little earlier. One evening Suvi called me and told me to meet her at the hostel as she wanted some time alone with me. I met her.

"What is with you and Abhi? You're acting like an ice maiden. I hope you know that," she said.

"What ice maiden? What do you want me to do? Write him a love letter in blood?" I retorted a bit sharply.

"Come on Anks. Haven't you seen the way he looks at you like a lost puppy? Don't tell me your ambitions have blinded you that much that you can't see."

"God, you too! What *is* with you guys? Just because I made it and you all didn't, do I have to be penalised? Where have I become blind? And what does my ambition have anything to do with it?"

"You idiot, you aren't even trying to understand what I' m trying to say. It is wrong if you keep behaving like this. At least talk to Abhi. Explain to him properly. You owe him that much. If you want to end it, end it. But don't keeping him dangling like this. It is cruel, Anks," she said it slowly and patiently like explaining to a child and that strangely calmed me down too.

"Suvi, I have really tried. He wants me to do MBA at CUSAT along with him. How can I? What kind of madness is that? Firstly I don't want to and even if by the remotest chance, I did agree, what in the world will I tell my parents? Has he thought of that?" I asked her.

"I think you do need to meet him once and have a heart to heart chat. That should clear things up," she said.

I decided I would. I had also been uncomfortable playing this peek-a-boo game with him, talking but not communicating. It was high time to end this juvenile nonsense.

I called up Abhi one evening when my parents weren't at home. They were busy these days and often went out as they had a number of things to do before we relocated in Bombay. Abhi's grandfather answered the phone. I introduced myself and of course he remembered me.

"How lovely to hear from you, *Molle* ! Please hold on, I'll tell Abhi to pick it up in his room," he said, using the Malayalam term affectionately which was the equivalent of '*beti*' in Hindi. I found this gesture of his charming and I also realised that in his own discreet way he was trying to tell me that Abhi would be talking from his room, and therefore we had the privacy. I was moved by his sensitivity and envied Abhi a bit, for this easy relationship that he had with his grandpa.

"Hey," I said when Abhi answered.

"Anks!" he exclaimed, taken completely by surprise, the joy evident in his voice. "Wow, wow! Look who is calling me! And before you say anything I am so so sorry. You did not even listen to me and I did call you thrice to explain. I spoke all three times to your mum."

"No apologies needed and you should know by now that if you spoke to my mom, I would never get the message. I am surprised she wasn't curt with you."

"She was but I would not give up. And I didn't want to mention all this in front of others and so never really got a chance to tell you this."

"Yes, thanks for that. Look, we must meet. I want to talk to you."

"Of course, Madam! Anytime, any place. Your wish is my command," he said. The happiness in his voice almost broke my heart.

I silently cursed Suvi. It was her bright idea, meeting him. The earlier situation was definitely easier. We could have maintained that and then slowly I would have moved to Bombay and we could have drifted apart naturally. This was painful. There was a lump in my throat at the genuine thrill and eagerness in his voice.

"Do you want to meet at my place?" he asked.

"No," I said. I could not stand the intimacy of his room and breaking it to him at his own place sounded very cruel to me. "Let us meet in the morning tomorrow at Appu's. No one is around in the mornings, there." I said.

"Ok, Appu's it is. At ten?" he asked.

"Yes, I'll be there," I said.

"I'll be there before you and hey Ankita, I love you," he said and the tenderness in his voice felt like a jab in the pit of my stomach.

"Bye," I said as I hung up.

True to his word, he was waiting when I reached. He jumped up as soon as he saw me and planted a kiss on my cheek.

"Abhi! What are you doing?! This is a public place!" I said shocked at his action. In a place like Cochin, a girl talking to a boy alone at a public place itself was really not acceptable. An action like this was the worst crime a guy and a girl could commit. I quickly looked around to see if anyone had noticed and heaved a sigh of relief to see that the place was quite deserted.

"I could not help it Anks, you look so lovely!"

We sat in the shade, looking at the clear blue water sparkling and shining, with ships and boats in the back ground, sailing away to far off lands.

"So, say! Why did you want to meet me?" asked Abhi. His eyes were still shining with love and the shadows of the trees were making criss-crosses on his face.

Love, whatever form it takes, is a funny thing indeed. I knew at that moment that I could not tell him what I really wanted to say. At least not today, not now, I decided.

"Just like that. We have hardly met after that day. So I thought we could spend some time together," I said. I knew I was being a coward. My inner voice taunted me to go ahead and tell him that it was over. I could not.

"Oh Ankita, I am so happy now. You know, I haven't been sleeping well the last few days because I felt the distance was growing between us. But today I know, it does not matter. All that matters is now."

"Yes, God knows when we will meet, once I move to Bombay," I said as gently as I could. I had to bring him back to reality.

"So, you are hell bent on that?"

"I have told you Abhi. There is no reason I can give my parents which is valid enough for me to stay back in Cochin and you know that. Let us not start this again, please."

"Ankita, Marry me! Let us get married before you go." said Abhi.

I was totally taken by surprise. Was he crazy?! Had he lost it?

"What are you saying, Abhi? Are you serious?!" I exclaimed, shocked for the second time that day.

"Look, I have thought about it. It can be a secret court marriage. Do you know Naina and Yamin? They did that. And you know what—their parents don't even know. Once Yamin gets a job, they intend telling their parents. Till then they are staying apart and meeting every day at college and everything goes on like normal," he said.

I knew about Naina and Yamin who were second year post graduate students at Mahaveers. But I did not have any inkling of their secret marriage.

"What?! They are married?" I exclaimed.

He nodded. "Well, they're both over 21 and you just need a month's time and two witnesses. In fact, even a month is not needed if you know the right people. And I know whose palms to grease. Being in college politics teaches you a lot," he said matter-of-factly.

This was getting out of hand and in a direction I had not anticipated.

"Come on Abhi. We can't possibly do that," I stalled for time, thinking of what to say.

"Oh yes, we can. Why not? There are those who look at things the way they are and ask why. I dream of things that never were and ask why not. Why not? Why not?" he said, quoting Kennedy.

Because it must have been love but it is over now.

But somehow matching Kennedy's quote with a song from Roxette, especially at that moment seemed dastardly and I backed out. Instead, I matched it with a quote I remembered.

"Adopt the pace of nature. Her secret is patience," I said ambiguously. "Ralph Waldo Emerson, in case you did not know," I added.

He smiled. "I am willing to wait a lifetime for you Ankita, if you will say yes."

How could I promise? How could I tell him that my dreams had grown beyond the town of Cochin? They had tasted life outside. They had seen a wider world out there. I wanted a slice of that. It was mine for the asking. I could not be tied down like this. I could not commit. I could not give him my word. Heck, I could not even tell him that I loved him.

"Oh Abhi. I can't promise anything. I wish I could." I said, hating myself as I said it. But there it was. Out in the open. It was the truth and it hung in the air like a shroud.

He looked crestfallen. He did not speak for what seemed like a long time.

I looked away and stared at the sea. I did not know what to say to make this blow gentler.

When he finally spoke, his words were a whisper. "At least keep in touch, that is all I ask," he said. "That is all I ask."

The depth of those words would hit me only years later after I had undergone a lot more and after I had been wiser. That time I had not even said I would because I really did not know and saying things like these seemed a bit silly. We had bid good bye to each other. In the years to come, I would replay this scene in my mind over and over, again and again, his words echoing in my ears.

The next day was a Sunday and my parents again had a round of relatives to visit. I was getting tired of it and opted to stay at home. That was when I got the phone call from Suvi.

"Hey, what in the world happened between you and Abhi? Did you spend the night with him?" she asked. She knew I would be meeting him but I had not spoken to her after that.

"Are you crazy? Won't I tell you if I did? You forget that I don't live in the hostel and am accountable to my parents. Are you calling to ask me to ask this absurd question?"

"No, you ass. Abhi has been missing from home since last morning. He did not go home in the night. Dhiren just called me. Abhi's grandfather is frantic. The police are searching for him. His dad has been informed too."

"Oh my God," I said. "No, I have no idea. Last I saw him was yesterday morning."

I didn't know what to do. I wanted to call up his grandfather and tell him what had happened between Abhi and me the previous morning. But that would not have helped at all. Maybe he was spending the night at a friend's and had got drunk and therefore not called his grandpa, I thought. But it sounded hollow to my own ears. Abhi was never like that. He was responsible and loved his grandpa far too much. A drink or two would have never been a problem in facing his grandfather, I knew. There was nothing I could do to fight that sinking feeling which was beginning to creep up and soak me like cold water that has spilled on a chair and which you have inadvertently sat upon.

It was my mother who broke the news to me the next day. It was all over the newspapers.

"Did you know this chap? What a pity. They recovered his body in Vypeen. So young, I don't know why these people drink." she said as she handed me the newspaper.

The sinking feeling had grown to a giant wave and I was submerged in it completely now. I was too stunned to react. I read the report which said that his bike and an empty bottle of whiskey were recovered from the beach at Fort Kochi by the police. They had traced the bike the previous day itself. But it was only late last evening that the body had washed ashore, miles away in Vypeen which was a neighbouring town.

They say when a calamity strikes you it stuns your normal senses so much that emotions are held in check. Perhaps that is what happened with me.

"Yes, I know him. I have seen him at youth festivals," I heard myself saying calmly to my mom, handing her back the newspaper. I was surprised at my own clever line which was not completely a lie too.

I went to my room and sat on my bed, my heart beats pounding away like an overworked pump. I was numb with pain. I had to see Suvi. I could not handle this on my own. I managed to put up a nonchalant facade as I told my mom that I was going out for the day and called Suvi.

She was waiting at the hostel gate and she hugged me tight as soon as she saw me. Then we made our way towards the arches. It was only then that I finally broke down. Between sobs I told her what had happened the previous day. My nose was running and I was crying and wiping it on my sleeve. I was beyond caring.

I told Suvi that I just had to speak to his grandfather now. I did not trust myself to talk. We made our way to a phone booth just outside the college gates. I asked her to ask for him and then hand me the phone when he came on line. I heard her asking in Malayalam for Abhi's *appachan*.

When he came on the line I did not know what to say.

"Hello, this is Ankita, Abhi's friend," I said stupidly.

"*Molle*," he said his voice full of anguish. "I know he loved you. I don't know what happened between you two, but I have only one thing to say. You are young, you are pretty. Please remember *molle, sneham mathram puchikaruthu.* No matter from where it comes," and he wept. The sound of a grown up man crying is one of the loneliest, saddest sounds I have ever heard. The words he said in Malayalam singed and burnt a hole in my soul. I would never ever forget those words or his voice my entire life. "Never belittle love," is the closest translation that I can come up with for the words he spoke that day.

He went on to say that the police had been around earlier and had specifically asked if he was romantically involved with anybody. They had said that suicide cases due to 'love-affairs' were common. His grandfather told me that Abhi would never have wanted my name dragged in and so he gave his statement on record, that there was no such thing as far as he knew. Silently and selfishly I thanked the largeness of his heart. I cried some more, but only after I had hung up.

The post mortem reports concluded death by drowning with high levels of alcohol as a contributing factor. The funeral procession was the next day.

I did not go for the funeral. I told Suvi that I couldn't come. She tried persuading me. I would not budge from my decision.

"I don't want to see a bloated dead body. I have seen him when he was alive and well and those shall be my last memories." I said. I hated myself for it. Yet I could not bring myself to go.

I wondered why he had drunk so much. Did the tide rise and then he was so drunk that he did not notice? Had he been washed away and it was too late? Had he screamed for help in the night? Did his screams ring out? Why had he done such a foolish thing as drinking alone on the beach? My inner voice was screaming out the answers blaming me.

But I silenced it, not allowing it to rise up, not wanting to hear it.

I wished I had told him that I would keep in touch. I wished I had told him that a part of me loved him. I wish I had assured him that we would meet when I visited Cochin once a year for holidays. I wished a hundred million times. I wished a hundred million things.

They remained just wishes which would taunt me all my life and which had taught me an important lesson which would stay with me for as long as I lived and shape all my future dealing with people—Never to belittle love, no matter where it came from and to be a little humbler, nicer and kinder with my words and actions.

10

Racing ahead

Bombay is everything I imagined it to be and everything I never imagine it to be too. Bombay is like the proverbial elephant being described by five blind men. Everyone feels a tiny bit of it and is convinced that their version of it is the real Bombay.

It was a giant cauldron of cultures, personalities, pockets and they blended effortlessly merging to create a new pot-pourri which welcomed everybody. It was almost magical. No matter which part of the country you came from, no matter whether you were a foreigner or a native, no matter what you wore or how you spoke, Bombay quietly understood, accepted and welcomed you into its fold. You felt right at home and you fitted in.

In Bombay, people measured distances by time taken to commute. The suburban railway carried more than 6 million commuters on a daily basis. This was more than half the capacity of passengers on the Indian railways itself. I took to it, like a duck to water and became just one passenger in the 6 million. There were about 60 of us in my batch. The Institute did not have its own hostels but those students who were from outside, were accommodated in the Bombay University hostels. Others were mostly day scholars and just used the local trains.

On most days, I would leave home at 7.A.M as it took me a about an hour and twenty minutes to get to college. I learnt to manage the commute, in no time at all.

At my new college, everybody went all out to welcome us, the freshmen. The Dean, the Director and two other professors addressed us. They said the usual things that are said on such occasions. They talked about how this was the first step in a new journey, how we would be transformed at the end of the course and how we would lead and take our places in the corporate world. They spoke about the glory of the Institute. They gave us an outline of what to expect. Then there was a slide show. There was one slide which made us feel very important— they had calculated the number of people who had applied and the number that finally got selected and told us the probability of getting selected and that we were in a privileged fraction. They made us feel special and a part of an elite family. After this we took a break for snacks and refreshments.

The second part of the session was an Ice breaking session. They had put all our names into a bowl and drew out five at a time, and the five that they drew out formed a group. There were only twelve girls in my class. The men far outnumbered the women. By a strange quirk, my group had three girls including myself. All the other groups had just one girl or were all-male. The two boys who were in our group were getting undisguised envious looks from other guys as if saying “Lucky dogs”. We were given time to discuss and prepare and we had to present a short ad film about our group, with slides, introducing each member, their likes, dislikes and anything else we thought relevant. They asked us to be as creative and different as we could. They gave us OHP sheets and markers and set us to work. Initially everyone seemed hesitant and lost, but gradually everyone started speaking and in no time there was laughter, ribbing and discussions as each group got involved in the task at hand.

The two girls in my group were Chaya and Jigna, both of whom had been born and brought up in Bombay. They presented a study in contrast. Chaya was thin and short and looked like a child who was in Class 10, not a student of a Management Institute. Jigna was very tall, fair and well built with short hair and very confident. I found the name Jigna to be very unusual and had to ask her twice what her name was. Jigna had no work experience like me and was fresh from college. But Chaya had been working with a financial firm for a year. Of the two guys, the first namely Joseph, looked like an absent minded professor. He had a mop of unruly curly hair and twinkling eyes. Joseph had worked for two years at a shipping firm. Uday was bearded and had an air of restlessness and arrogance about him. He was fresh from an engineering college but looked a lot older than a student who had just finished Engineering.

The classes at my new college began right in earnest.

My days at Agnes seemed like a different lifetime and a different world. It had been only about two months since I moved to Bombay but it felt like I had been here forever. Maybe it was my attitude or maybe it was the place, but I had taken to it marvellously and was completely at ease. I had made new friends too and I felt happy that I fitted in.

I had really begun to enjoy my course even though the methodology for teaching used in a Management School was different from anything I had experienced before. It was the first time I discovered that subjects could be taught without books or lectures, at least not the conventional way.

I heard from both Suvi and Vaibhav. I was delighted to get their letters and be back in touch.

It was around this time that I began to take an active interest in running. I do not know how it started, but suddenly I decided that I would begin jogging. I had always been actively involved in sports at school but I seemed to have forgotten it at college. I announced my intentions to my parents and kept the spare key to the house so that I would not disturb my parents when I went out. The residential complex I stayed in had a lovely jogging track and I would wake up at 5.00 A.M. and begin my day with a jog. It was invigorating. I felt full of energy and so lively as I began my day. Sights that I would normally not see—newspapers being stacked in piles, ready to be delivered, the milk sachets arriving, people walking their dogs, old people doing yoga in a group in the park—all this greeted me and I looked at it, marvelling that there was an entire new 'morning world' out there, right under my nose something that I had missed earlier.

When I reached college that day, Jigna and Joseph both remarked how charged up I was looking.

Later when we took a break for tea, Joseph took me aside and asked if I had been doing drugs.

"Oh no! I don't even smoke," I said and he laughed at how horrified I looked.

"Come on *yaar.* It is not as though it is the ultimate sin. You looked kind of manic, this morning." he said.

"It may not be the ultimate sin but it definitely is not for me. Maybe I am looking 'charged up', as you call it, because I have started jogging."

"Ah-ha! That explains it! It seems you have this store house of energy that you are waiting to unleash."

Later on the way home, I thought about what he said. It was the first time that someone had described me as manic. He was unwittingly very close to the truth, but of course at that time neither he nor I or anybody else in the world had even the slightest inkling or suspicion about it. On the surface I seemed normal. But underneath changes were taking place, so subtle, so gradual and slowly, much like the gradual movements in tectonic plates which would then result in a large outburst like a volcanic eruption. Had I known about it then, perhaps I could have taken a path that took a different turn. But nobody was aware, least of all me. If I had woken up one morning and found myself transformed into a completely different person, perhaps the change would have been obvious. It was a series of events that had to be pieced together gradually like a jigsaw puzzle and it was only when you finished the jigsaw that it made sense.

I began sleeping less and less. On most days I got home by 7.30 P.M or sometimes 8.00. My mother would always have a hot meal ready for me. She felt I was working very hard which I indeed was. After we had our meal together my parents would retire for the night. I would begin studying the books I had borrowed from the Institute library. It was like a whole new door had opened and there was so much to discover.

I began studying seriously. I started to make elaborate notes about everything I read. I felt that if I colour coded them I could remember it better. So I bought a pack of sketch pens and colour pencils. If there was a particular explanation I liked from a Philip Kotler book, I would write it in green. If there was an example which perfectly illustrated what had just been explained I would use an orange sketch pen and write it down. Surprisingly, the more I began writing in colours the more clear things began to become. I was delighted with this secret discovery of mine. It was as though I had suddenly discovered a magic power. The most amazing thing about it was that, the next day or even days after I wrote, I could instantly recall every single word down to the last detail. I had begun seeing words as visuals. I had always been very fast at reading. My verbal ability was one of my strengths which had helped me clear the entrance test, making up for my deficiency with numbers. But now it seemed to have improved three times. I felt like a monster devouring books. I was always hungry. I wanted more and more. This obsession would cost me dearly later. Things have a way of balancing out. But it felt so good and I was so exhilarated with the discovery of this 'power' that I did not want it to stop. It was almost as though I had a photographic memory. The passages I wrote were so clear in my mind. I could reproduce them almost verbatim. The bonus was that I perfectly understood all of it too. It was not that I was merely reproducing words without comprehending them. I could close my eyes and clearly see the pages and pages of notes I had made in colour. The images were indeed like photographs and I seem to keep clicking mental pictures. What I had not anticipated was running out of film.

Most days I would be studying way past 2.00.A.M. I was so excited at the prospect of studying and learning even more things than I already knew that I just could not sleep. By 5.00.A.M, the next morning, I was up again, back to my jogging track. As I jogged I would recall everything I read the previous night and everything I had made notes about. My notes began increasing rapidly and I filed them neatly. Sometimes in the margins I drew pictures that would help me remember what I had read. I made acronyms which would help me in recalling almost all the points that explained a particular concept. Perhaps it was a way of exorcising Abhi's memories or perhaps it was my enthusiasm to excel which made me work so hard, I don't know. Whatever it was, it seemed to be propelling me forward and pushing me to work harder and harder.

After I got back from my jog, I would rush to college. My parents were happy to see me working so much. If they knew what was to come later they would have probably stopped me. But they did not and they felt very proud of their 'star-child'.

My stamina began to improve dramatically. I could jog great distances without going out of breath. I was no longer satisfied with slow jogging. I started practising sprints. One morning I wanted to see how fast I could run. I wanted to measure the distance and I had no measuring tape. My watch had a stop-watch function and I timed myself. When I finished I was astonished to see that I could run 100 metres in about 13.8 seconds. I was certain that it was close to the national record. This discovery gave me such a thrill that I just could not keep quiet about it. When I came home I told my parents about it.

My mother said "I think you should stop this jogging of yours. Look at you. You have become so thin. You look like someone who escaped from a concentration camp."

I was irritated with my mother but I chose to keep quiet. Afterwards, I looked at myself in a full length mirror. My mother did have a point. I was shocked to see how thin I had become. But I consoled myself saying one could never be too thin or too rich.

Later, when I met my friends I could not contain my discovery about my running speed. I told Joseph, Chaya and Jigna about it.

"Hail! Here is India's next P.T. Usha," said Joseph and the others sniggered.

"Come on guys. Time me. I will prove it," I said.

A lot of people had gathered to watch the challenge. I was certain I could do it. Joseph had measured the 100 metre distance in the open quadrangle of the Institute and set the starting and finishing marks.

Jigna was at the start. She said "Ready, steady and go" and I sprinted.

I completed it in 13.8 seconds.

"*Arre. Yeh sach mein PT. Usha nikli boss!*" Joseph exclaimed.

I walked up to Joseph and said in a quiet voice, "Don't ever fucking doubt what I say in future? Got it?" There was an edge in my voice which was alien to me. I had no idea why I was seething and aggressive. It was as though I wanted to strike him. I could suddenly see the concern and slight fear in his eyes. Everybody was quiet. It seemed very funny and I started laughing uncontrollably. There was silence for a fraction of a second and then all of them joined in the laughter and the moment passed off as a joke. But I sensed something in me close to snapping at that point in time. But as was my usual way, I brushed it aside.

I.T or information technology was one of the subjects in the course. We had an exam coming up soon. I studied like a maniac. I had made extensive notes again in colour. When the results came out a week later, I had topped the class. I had scored a ninety eight out of hundred. The person who came second was Uday and he had scored only seventy six. The Faculty who taught the course was very impressed with me. But I was far from happy. I kept looking at the paper and kept getting angry that I had lost two marks. It was as if I was possessed by a spirit of perfection.

"I like your attitude. Very well done," said Sushil Mehra, the faculty for the course. He was very young and everybody called him Sushil.

"But Sushil, I was expecting a centum," I said, the disappointment showing in my voice.

"Next time, Ankita," he smiled.

There was to be no next time. This was the zenith, the pinnacle. There would be more mountains to climb but of a different kind. But to climb those I had to descend first.

But before I descended I would stun everybody including myself. The chain of events that happened at the first Inter collegiate event in my new course was the backdrop to it.

That was to come later. For now I was content and secure basking in the glory of my academic success and my daily running.

11

Dancing in the dark

The cultural festival was exactly like the numerous ones I had attended in my previous college but it was not competitive at all. It was more for fun and entertainment. Yet it had a lot of corporate sponsors. I was told that it gave the seniors a good working experience to organise such events.

When we entered the venue, I was dazzled by the flamboyant way it was done up. The glitter, glamour and the stylish way the compere was addressing everyone, the huge speakers and the shiny ball in the centre suspended from the ceiling which reflected disco lights, the dance floor, the stage, the corporate banners that blended in seamlessly and smoothly, were all well integrated.

Chaya, Jigna, Uday and Joseph too were impressed. We were a little late and it had already begun. The compere was now announcing the next contest which was popularly called JAM or 'Just a minute'.

"You must take part in this," Joseph said.

The Compere was calling for entries and before I could protest to

Joseph, he caught my hand and raised it high, calling out my name. She immediately announced it on the mike and I had no option but to go up on stage.

Standing on that stage with the spotlight focussed on me I felt a strange sense of exhilaration. A million thoughts were swarming in my mind like a pack of bees whose beehive has been disturbed. I struggled to rein them in. They were floating across in hordes and my mind struggled to keep up the pace. I tried to slow down my thinking, tried to desperately make sense of what I was feeling but the more I tried the more aware I became that I couldn't. A sense of ecstatic feeling was washing over me in waves.

I was aware of the compere now pushing a bowl towards me which held bits of paper that had the topic for JAM written on them. I took out one and opened it. It read "Clint Eastwood's drinking preference Good Vodka, Bad Martini and Ugly Rum." I had ten seconds to compose my thoughts and then I would have to speak on the topic without a pause, a stammer, a stutter or a grammatical error. The theme sound track from the motion picture 'Good, Bad and Ugly' started playing and suddenly every note in the music that was playing in the background became so poignant, so clear and so very intense.

As the music faded I started speaking about how Ms. Martini, Ms. Vodka and Ms. Rum were actually three ladies who had a crush on Eastwood and how their styles of sipping alcohol affected their relationship with Eastwood. I spoke effortlessly and my speech was full of sexual innuendos and I had the audience roaring with laughter. I felt supremely charged up with my own cleverness and stunned myself by speaking so clearly and so engagingly that the compere forgot to ring the bell at the end of one minute. I continued for a full three minutes, before she realised and then interrupted me and announced my amazing performance. By now the audience was screaming "More! More! Let her continue. We want to hear more." I grabbed the mike from the compere and continued for two more minutes. I was feeling invincible, irresistible, charming and at the top of the world. When I stepped off the stage, with thunderous applause resounding in my ears, Joseph came and hugged me and carried me in the air and I squealed in delight as I told him to put me down. Chaya, Jigna and Uday crowded around me and looked at me with awe.

"Oh my God! You are really too good *yaar*. We had no idea you were that good!" said Jigna.

The music now changed to dance music and alcohol and starters were being served. The rest of the evening was purely party time and people had already begun dancing. I suddenly wanted to dance. I was never one to be this enthusiastic and usually preferred to be a bystander, but I seemed to have transformed entirely that night. It was as if a different person had completely taken over me.

"Come on, let us dance," I told Joseph who was surprised as I pulled him towards the dance floor and we began dancing. It was as if I had drunk a lot but the truth was I had not touched a drop of alcohol. I was dancing with wild abandon and gyrating wildly. The music playing was a Samba number and it perfectly matched my upbeat, frenzied mood. I realised I was feeling flirtatious and I danced close to Joseph for a long time. I could see he was thoroughly enjoying it and at one point he had his hands snaked around my waist. I felt seductive, attractive and experienced a sense of profound joy. Each rhythm and beat, each note, each sound of music became crystal clear to me and I could suddenly feel the piercing beauty of each individual note. My body seemed to have got a super charge and the ones around me seemed to feel my magnetism too.

We finally stopped after a long time. Then Joseph asked me if I wanted to go up to the terrace. He said the view was marvellous.

I agreed immediately without much thought. I could see Chaya dancing at the other end of the dance floor. Jigna was enjoying a drink and talking to a guy I did not recognise. I gestured to her that I was going upstairs. She nodded absent-mindedly.

Joseph and I made our way upstairs, through a narrow set of stairs. As we went up, the cool night breeze hit my face. There seemed to be a million stars in the sky. We could hear the music from downstairs very clearly.

I looked around the terrace and found that many people were sitting around. Some couples were making out. Some stood at the edge of the parapet, looking around at the millions of twinkling lights that looked as magnificent as the stars in the sky. The city stretched out for miles around, spread out like a magic carpet, it's ugly underbelly, crowded buildings, streets, sprawling slums and millions of people cloaked by the magic darkness of the night studded with glowing city lights , unaware of the happenings on top of this single building that was a part of its thousands.

I looked to the side and could see Uday and a group of guys. Uday was sitting, leaning his back against a water tank like structure, made of concrete. He seemed to be unnaturally still and that was when I noticed a syringe planted in his elbow and he was slowly pushing the plunger in. I looked at Joseph and saw that he had noticed it too.

"Do you want to try?" he asked.

A strange sense of absolute assuredness combined with a manic wild abandon was engulfing me now. It was nothing like I had ever felt before.

"No, but I want to dance."

"Shall we go back to the dance floor?" asked Joseph. He had his hands around my waist, from the back now, like he was my boyfriend and funnily I did not care. In fact I liked it that he was being protective towards me.

"No, I want to dance now," I said and before he could say anything, I had reached over to the parapet, climbed on top of it and started balancing precariously over the edge.

I saw the shock and fear in Joseph's eyes. It made me laugh and it compelled me to shock him more. I was oblivious of the danger. I was immune to the fact that death was certain if I fell backwards, a drop of more than 10 floors. I was enjoying it immensely and feeling indomitably powerful.

"Anks—what the hell are you doing? GET DOWN RIGHT NOW," Joseph screamed.

Several people turned to look. It goaded me on even more.

"It would be marvellous to jump, won't it?" I laughed again, now a little uncontrollably.

"Anks—that is quite enough, Please come down now. Please. I beg you" said Joseph and I could hear the fear and desperation his voice.

"What has she been taking? Which idiot let her have it? " asked a guy whom I had never seen before.

Suddenly I felt a bolt of anger shooting up inside me. How dare this imbecile even imply I was drugged? I had not even taken a drop of alcohol. I felt violence surging inside me like a wave and suddenly

I wanted to hit him. I jumped off the parapet towards him.

"Who the fuck, are you?" I shouted at him as I advanced towards him. He took a step backwards, clearly taken aback and it enraged me further. I went towards him and grabbed his collar.

"Do you fucking know? Have you fucking seen me doing drugs or drinking?" I was shaking him now and he did not know what to do. Expletives were flowing from my mouth like water, something that wasn't what I did normally. It was as though I had no control over what I was saying anymore. I could see alarm rising in him and again I was finding that funny. I wanted to laugh, but by then Joseph had grabbed me from behind.

"That is enough. Come, let us go downstairs," he said. It seemed as if he was frightened even to say anything to me.

I turned around and saw Uday watching the whole thing impassively. Jigna and Chaya too were on the terrace now. I had no idea when they had come up but judging by the looks on their faces, it was evident they had witnessed a lot of the drama that had just unfolded. I could see concern in their faces now.

"It is okay, I am fine" I assured Chaya though I had no idea what had just happened and why I had behaved like that.

"Umm, tell the truth. Were you drinking? Or have you taken something? Did Uday give you a fix?" asked Joseph.

"No, I haven't. Haven't I been with you whole evening? Come on guys. I thought at least all of you know me," I said, a little offended.

"It seems like I really don't know you Ankita. You're full of surprises today. Anyway, you managed to scare me stiff," said Joseph and he was looking at me strangely now, as though seeing me for the first time.

"Sorry, it was just a bit of harmless fun. I guess I went a little overboard," I said half contritely now, sensing that they were really concerned.

We took the train back to Chaya's home. Joseph and another guy from our class saw us off at the station. Joseph asked if he should accompany us. Chaya assured him that we would be fine.

Later that night, Chaya and I spread out a mattress in her drawing room. Her parents were already asleep in their cramped one bedroom apartment. Her brother and grandmother too were asleep in one corner of the drawing room. They were very used to sharing spaces.

"Hey Anks," whispered Chaya as we lay down "Don't take such risks again. What if you had fallen over?" she asked.

I could not answer her. I had no idea myself what I had been doing. It was the first time in my life that I realised that I could not trust my own self anymore. It was a very terrifying thought. I blinked away tears of shame that had been welling up in my eyes and threatening to fall. Then I turned over to the other side and pretended to be asleep though it was a very long time, probably hours before I managed to fall asleep.

12

The descent

We had a test on Monday morning. Professor, R.S.V. Murthy who taught the course was not one of my favourites. I hated his sarcasm and his know-it-all attitude. Almost everybody disliked him and he was nicknamed MM, which our seniors proudly clarified, stood for '*Moorkh* Murthy' and not 'marketing management' which was the subject he taught. MM quoted extensively and almost verbatim from a management book by Philip Kotler. Most of the people in my class had perfected the art of sleeping with their eyes open, thanks to this Professor. His nasal drone set the right mood for a snooze and many a time I had to nudge Uday, as he would slump on his desk and doze off. There was nothing of value in whatever the professor said. He might as well have been playing a taped version of someone reading out passages from Kotler's book.

I could almost predict what the questions for the test would be. I had borrowed Kotler from the Institute library. I had already gone through the book and made extensive notes, using the same colour coded technique that I had used earlier for preparing notes. When I closed the book, I visualised it and just as it had been earlier, I could recall every single word, like a photograph, inside my mind. I was very pleased. Then I decided to go one step further. I wrote out the question paper, anticipating the questions that MM would set. I went ahead and wrote out the answers without looking into the book. When I compared the text book to the answers I had written, I was even more pleased. They were almost exactly alike and nobody would have believed that they had not been copied, but written out from memory. To top it, I had written not only definitions and jargon from the book but had also added my own detailed analysis as well. When I read the paper, I knew it would be graded a straight A.

Suddenly I was overcome with an overwhelming urge to share this with everybody in my class. I decided to photocopy it and distribute it. I hurried towards the nearest photocopying centre. When I reached there, I told the guy who operated the machine that I wanted about seventy copies. He was a little surprised.

"Madam seventy or seventeen?" he asked.

I clarified it was indeed seventy. I felt that I could distribute it to various professors too as well as the Dean. I felt it was a wonderful idea as they would see that was happening in MM's course. I felt it would be an eye-opener. I wanted to share my 'colour coded' way of remembering things with everybody, so they too could benefit. I felt like I had stumbled upon a great secret and my discovery would be hailed. I pictured it being used in schools, colleges and everywhere else as a new memory technique. I wondered why nobody else had thought of such a simple but brilliant technique earlier. As I was waiting for him to finish making the photocopies, my eyes chanced upon small glittering stickers of cartoon characters like Tweety bird, Fairies and Garfield and some Disney characters, which children use to decorate their books and other objects. I thought the stickers would make a nice finishing touch and I bought twenty sheets. I also came across some very beautiful printed stationery and could not resist buying about eight packets of writing sheets. They looked very beautiful and I decided I would surprise Suvi and Vaibhav with letters. I also looked around the shop and discovered some water colours. I had last painted with water colours only in school. On an impulse, I bought a set of water colours and a set of brushes as well. It was like an urgent impulse inside my head that was driving me to buy all this stuff. They seemed *absolutely* essential.

I reached home armed with my large bag of purchases and unpacked them carefully and arranged them all on my desk. Then I sat down and decorated the corners of each set of notes with tiny stickers of cartoon characters. I used highlighter pens and highlighted each set of the notes in my colour coded way with green, purple and orange. There were seventy sets to finish and I was like a woman possessed. I stayed up the whole night doing just this. I was a reservoir of energy. I just couldn't stop. Strangely I did not feel even a little tired. By the time I finished it was already 7.00.a.m and it was time to leave for college. I made myself a strong cup of black coffee and two scrambled eggs, and rushed out hurriedly. I did not even realise that I had not slept the whole night.

When I reached college, I began distributing the notes I had painstakingly photocopied and colour coded and also decorated with stickers. Everyone gathered around me like bees around a honeycomb, as I began giving out the notes. It caused a stir in the campus.

"Oh my God—look at this!" said one.

"Did you do all of them?" asked another

"But why?!" said a third shaking his head in amazement.

"Oh! Look at those stickers! So cute!" screeched a female voice.

I could see they were very pleased and very surprised too.

Joseph was amazed and astonished. But he caught hold of me by my elbow and took me aside. I still clutched a few copies of my notes in my hand which I intended giving to the Dean and MM.

"Ankita, Are you ok? You have that same look in your eyes which you had earlier."

"What look Jo? I am fine! I wrote it all myself, that too without consulting the book," I said proudly, a bit exasperated and annoyed that he did not appreciate my action instantly. "I am going to give a copy to the Dean and to MM too. Let them know how predictable a paper he sets. It is time someone opened their eyes," I said.

He shook his head, clearly displeased. "And are you going to be their eye opener? Come on Anks. Have some sense."

"What is wrong, Jo? I want the Dean to know what is going on."

"No, I won't let you. This thing you have done, distributing notes like this, is crazy enough. Come now, let us go and give the test," he said firmly, walking me away from the crowd and in the direction of the classrooms.

He had uncannily spoken the truth about my actions being crazy, but the implications of it, were yet to sink in then.

The test was predictable and I sailed through it. I wrote out the answers almost effortlessly. I could hear a buzz when the question paper was given out. I wondered why the others could not have predicted the questions the way I had. If only they followed my colour coded system, they too would sail through.

After the class, many of my classmates thanked me for the notes.

Chaya and Jigna asked me why I had done it.

"Honestly, it all came easily to me and I felt like sharing," I said.

"Next time share only with us, your friends. Don't give the whole class. At least let us reap the rewards of our loyalty to you! We bow to you, Ankita the memory machine," quipped Uday, as I smiled and hit him on the head with a book. The others laughed too.

When I reached home I felt very pleased with myself. Everything around me seemed to have taken a new meaning which I seemed not to have appreciated earlier. Suddenly the garden in the residential complex I lived in looked so vibrant and so green. Each plant looked vivid. Each fern, each blade of grass, each flower had suddenly assumed amazing clarity and depth of colour. I was filled with an urgent sense of wonderment and beauty. The whole complex had a nicely landscaped garden filled with cobbled curving paths, a wooden bridge, manicured tended lawns and the focal point was a waterfall which looked so natural that it was almost impossible to make out that it was man made and had not existed there for centuries. It was a quiet shady brook and I was suddenly drawn to it as I gazed at it from the balcony in my room. I had seen this many times before but I had been so busy with my studies that I had never really paid attention to it. The more I gazed at it, the more alluring it felt. I realised that I had been truly blind all this while and was filled with a deep sense of regret. Then I wanted to capture its beauty forever on paper. Armed with my newly bought Art supplies, paints and brushes, I made my way towards the waterfall.

My mother called out to me and asked me where I was going and I told her that I was just going for a walk. A strange sense of peace and calmness enveloped me as I sat in front of the water fall and painted it. It had been years since I had held a paint brush. A group of children were playing in the garden and when they saw me painting they gathered around me. I did not mind the intrusion.

I stared at my work and stared at the waterfall. The more I looked at it the angrier I became, the earlier sense of peace that had surrounded me, quickly evaporating like water droplets on a sizzling hot griddle. I became angry that it was man made and not real. "At first they cut down trees to construct buildings and then they try and emulate nature," I thought angrily.

Then I took out my paint brush and wrote at the bottom of my picture "SHAMMING—MOTHER NATURE". I signed my name underneath and now was quite pleased with the end result. The more I looked at the picture, the more profoundness I could see in it. Again I was filled with a sense of loss, a terrible sadness and I began crying softly. I was a vortex of emotions. I felt Abhi would have understood perfectly what I had just realised and witnessed. It had been months since I had thought about Abhi, since that fateful day. Now I just could not stop. I yearned to talk to him. I wanted to hear his voice. I wanted to hold his hand. I wanted to see him smile and I wanted just once to press my lips against his. I remembered his words that day when I had last seen him, imploring me to keep in touch. I wished I had told him I would. I wished I had told him that Bombay wasn't far away and we could meet in the holidays and I could even do my summer project in Cochin. I wished I had assured him. But I had been too practical and too besotted with my own dreams back then.

The pain I was now feeling was almost physical. It felt like there was somebody inside my heart digging out little bits of it with a scalpel and throwing it away, a sense of emptiness quickly filling up the dugout bits. I was aching for Abhi. It was a longing which I had not allowed myself to feel. I did not know what to do, as I made my way home.

Then I felt that writing to Suvi would help. I took out the new stationary I had bought. I began writing. Words poured out like a flood. I wrote about meeting Abhi that last day, I wrote about the time during the youth festival when Abhi and I had first kissed, I wrote about the waterfall that I had just painted. I wrote about every little detail that I could remember about Abhi. I searched my mind, going down the annals of memory, digging out every little thing he had said, every place we had gone to, the things he had done, the expressions he had used, the way he had said them, the plans we had made. It all seemed terribly important that I write it to Suvi. I wrote and wrote and poured out my twenty one year old heart into those pages. When I finished I was shocked to look at the clock and see that it was nearly 5.00 A.M. I had once again stayed up the whole night without even realising it. I was even more shocked to see the length of my letter. It ran to forty two pages. I read it twice. Then I put it in an envelope and carefully wrote out her address so that I could mail it on the way to college.

I had no idea when I sent it off to her that it would later find its way into the hands of doctors. The psychiatrists would read it, dissect it, take it apart bit by bit and perhaps be privately amused by its contents, later label it as 'Incoherent and delusional ramblings caused due to mania or psychosis' and then would look for clues of a thought disorder. I did not even imagine that my grief, my pain and my seriousness poured out into those pages would be stripped bare and examined harshly under the blinding, unbearable glare of medical terminology and jargon, which I had not even heard of. In the harshness of that examination, my carefully chosen words full of angst, longing and sincerity would wilt and wane. They would be killed and stamped out. Not a trace would be left.

It was the first step that I had taken into descent. The irony was that I had thought it would soothe me, when I wrote it. I had no idea it would snake around my neck and form a noose which would almost take my life.

And the descent had just begun.

13

A stop gap relationship

Writing to Suvi, seemed to have awakened in me another kind of monster—that of writing. The amount of relief and satisfaction I felt after writing to her, had succeeded in giving me a feeling of re-assurance. It had helped me in keeping Abhi's memories alive. I could not write to Vaibhav about Abhi as I had never mentioned Abhi to him. I toyed with the idea of telling him everything starting from the beginning. Then when I thought about it, I felt he would never understand. So I wrote instead about my course, my college, my life in Bombay and my new found love for running. I also wrote about the colour coded way of remembering notes that I had discovered. I wrote in detail about the cultural festival but I left out the part where I had danced on the parapet. When I had finished, the letter ran to about 16 pages. I was satisfied and thought it would be a nice surprise for Vaibhav. I decorated the sides of the letters with hearts and tiny drawings. Then I added a few stickers too, left over from what I had used on the photocopies of the notes that I had distributed in college.

I was filled with a sense of impatience and urgency, like never before. Everything that I was doing had an impelling sense of having to be done immediately. I could not comprehend the reason for this, but if I wanted something I needed it immediately. It was now, now and now all the way that dominated my entire psyche and which kept me going, like a speeding train.

I was filled with so much of energy that I did not know what to do with it. Running around on my morning jogs, studying, devouring books, making huge amounts of detailed notes—I continued doing all of it with a burning frenzy. Nothing helped to expend it. My reserve was endless.

On many days I did not sleep at all. Thoughts raced around in my head like a colony of busy ants which had found a pile of food. I was filled with an almost coercive need to capture these thoughts somewhere. I bought a notebook and began writing in it. They were mostly poems. Words flowed like never before. I filled page after page with poetry about various things. On the left side of the book, I made drawings to go with them. I would sit up night after night, writing poetry. I would write about ordinary things, I would write about fantasy, about love and longing, about angst, about smells and sounds, I would write about the rains in Bombay—in short, I would write about anything that caught my fancy. I would use clever puns and rhymes. Sometimes the poems wouldn't rhyme at all but they would capture the essence of what I was trying to say. I would manipulate words and come up with what I thought were brilliant analogies. I thought my poetry was beautiful, sensitive and clever. But later the psychiatrists would examine these too like the letter and would look for clues to a thought disorder and would call it 'persistent disturbance to conscious thought, perhaps caused due to delusions'.

It would leave me sick to the pit of my stomach. Their conclusions and labelling would leave me so terrified and mentally scarred that it would be many years before I would be able to muster courage to even admit to anybody that I had written a poem. I would learn to stamp out any creativity and learn what 'normal' and 'appropriate' behaviour was. I would be filled with guilt and shake in fear if I wrote a poem. I would hide it like a criminal or tear it to bits, destroying evidence before I was discovered.

But I did not know any of that then and so I carried my little book with me everywhere I went and I wrote in it and drew to my heart's content whenever I felt like it.

It had been raining the whole morning that day and MM's class which was scheduled for the afternoon looked as drab as the muddy puddles that the rain had left outside.

"It is so boring! I really don't feel like attending," said Chaya, voicing out what all of us felt.

"Let us bunk then and go for a movie," I said.

"I checked. There is nothing good playing," replied Uday.

"Let us go somewhere then. How about the beach?" I suggested.

"In this rain? Are you crazy or what?" chimed Chaya, Uday and Jigna in unison.

Only Joseph did not say anything.

"So what if it is raining a bit? I think the ocean looks beautiful in the rain," I said, a little sulkily, annoyed that they could not appreciate my point of view.

"I agree," said Joseph, much to my surprise. "Come on Anks, let us go. Does anyone else want to come?" he asked.

Nobody did and so Joseph and I made our way, out of the Institute.

"Shall we walk to Marine Drive or do you want to take a cab?" he asked.

"Actually Jo, I have seen Marine drive so many times, but I have never been to Juhu beach."

"What? Despite being here for so many months, you haven't been there. What a shame! Let's go" said Joseph as he hailed a cab.

"Are we taking a cab all the way? Oh my God, it will cost so much. Let us wait for the bus."

"I am paying Anks, let me show you my city. Allow me, madam" he said, his voice filled with tenderness. When he looked at me, I was reminded of Abhi. I shuddered involuntarily. It was the same look that Abhi used to have when he looked at me.

In the cab, I sat in silence looking at Bombay in the rains. It was mesmerising. The monsoons lent everything a freshly washed look. Even the most common of city scenes seemed to have taken on a new beauty. A sense of longing and sadness washed over me. I fished out my notebook and without thinking began scribbling a poem. It was about nature weeping. Then I realised that Joseph was looking at me.

"Are you writing poetry?" he asked.

"Done now," I smiled as I folded the book and put it away.

"Let me see Anks, I want to read it," he said. He was whispering. He kept his left hand over my right hand which was resting on the seat of the cab. I made no attempt to move my hand away. We sat in silence, looking out. Then he held it and I turned towards him. He looked directly into my eyes. He raised my hand and kissed it. In that moment, for a fraction of a second, I saw Abhi instead of Joseph. Then the image was gone. I was filled with a longing and desperation of such intensity that I had never experienced before. My heart ached. My whole body ached. I could not stop tears from rolling down my cheeks.

Joseph was startled, "hey Anks, I am sorry! It is ok. You don't have to show me if you don't want to. I just asked. And I am so sorry I kissed your hand. I don't know what came over me. Sorry, sorry Anks."

"No, you idiot. It's not that," I said and I leaned towards him and kissed him on the lips, my tear soaked face, crushed against his. His stubble felt rough against my cheeks and I could smell his perfume which was a woody smell that I instantly liked. I inhaled deeply. I was kissing him for Abhi, I was kissing him as a repentance for never having admitted to Abhi that he did matter to me, I was kissing him because I could never kiss Abhi and I was hoping to fill that void that had been gnawing at my heart which I had managed to push aside every time. I felt no love for him, but I kissed him all the same, with a kind of fierceness and determination, as though to right the past, to bring back Abhi to life.

Joseph was abashed. But he looked very pleased too and suddenly very shy. The cab driver's eyes were popping out of his sockets as he got a clear view of what was happening in the passenger seat, in his rear view mirror.

"Anks! Not in the cab!" Joseph exclaimed

"Do you have another place in mind? If so we will go there." I teased and he guffawed.

I handed him my poetry book then. He took it like it was a treasure. He was silent as he read them one by one. He stroked the pages lovingly, running his hand over the drawings and over my hand-written words.

I nudged him when I saw the ocean. The skies were a turbulent grey and the sea danced in wild abandon. The wind sang a melancholy song as nature unfolded her splendour, like a dancer who knows that she is the cynosure of all eyes.

I watched enchanted and exclaimed "Oh Joseph, just look at it!"

Joseph told the cab driver to stop the cab as we made our way in the drizzle, to a restaurant that faced the beach. It was isolated at this hour, the weather contributing to it.

"Ankita, I am sure you have heard it many times before, but I must tell you this, you are really beautiful," said Joseph.

"Thanks Jo," I said as I saw Abhi in him again.

We spoke for a very long time sipping tea in the sea side cafe that day. Joseph told me about his childhood, about his growing up, about his dreams and hopes. He asked me about mine.

Somehow I did not want to tell him about Cochin or about Abhi. Abhi was like a precious secret that I was hugging to my chest. In a bizarre way, I felt that as long as I did not speak about Abhi I would be safe. Though what I needed the safety for I couldn't tell.

"I love you, Ankita," said Joseph finally.

I heard Abhi's grandfather's voice in my head and I heard his nerve wracking sobs. The recollection of that sound still singed my soul. I remembered what he said about never belittling love. I was silent for a while.

Then I said, "I love you Joseph."

But I did not mean it at all. I felt no love towards him. He was a nice guy, a great guy, a charming guy. But he was not for me. There was no way I was going to tell him that.

Later, I sat thinking in my room for a very long time. Thoughts spilled out, like an overstuffed sack of rice that had been punctured and the grains now scattered in all directions.

I loathed myself for lying to Joseph. I loathed myself for not having admitted the truth to Abhi . And I loathed myself for not being able to tell the whole truth to Vaibhav. I despised myself for getting involved with three different men. I looked at my face in the mirror. I hated it. I felt if I was ugly then they would not have told me I was beautiful and pretty. Maybe if I was ugly Abhi would still be alive. Maybe I could chop off my hair and make myself ugly. Maybe I could mutilate my face too. I hated it so much now.

That night too I did not sleep. I kept pacing up and down in my room. Vaibhav, Abhi and Joseph—their faces kept going round and round. What kind of a girl was I? How could I kiss Joseph like that? And how could I lie to him saying that I loved him? The thoughts kept going round and round like a whirlwind. They were spiralling wildly. There were various images coming into my head now and gambolling around the thoughts in perfect crescendo. I shut my eyes, trying to block them out. They would not go away.

They intensified so much that I finally I could not bear it any longer; I took out my poetry book and wrote the following poem:

A stop gap relationship

She looks at him with misty eyes

They have made love

Or attempted to

He seems content and relaxed

Most importantly, satisfied.

Not noticing her silence

Or perhaps choosing to ignore it

Not knowing its cause.

He is talking about leaving now
His voice a monotonous drone
Over the din of the fan in the background
In the cramped two room apartment
Filled with the smell of their sweating bodies.

In her mind a thought crosses
That the only difference between her
And her sisters on the street
The so called whores
Is that they receive payment in cash
And she receives it through emotions,
In form of words,
Words that have ceased to have a meaning now
Empty words—"I love you."

I read the poem I had just scribbled. The images I had just described in the poem had simply come into my head from nowhere.

The more I read the poem, the more I could relate to it. It made perfect sense to me.

Suddenly I realised why.

I felt a lot like the whore I had written about.

14

The day something died

It was now at least three weeks since I had slept properly. Even the times when I finally fell asleep, exhausted with all the myriad things I was involved in, it wasn't for more than a couple of hours. The thoughts raced around madly. I tried desperately to control them, to rein them in. They were like wild horses on a racing spree. The more I tried, the faster they seemed to gallop. At one point I was so exhausted I just wanted to sleep. I wanted to shout at the thoughts telling them to stop. I tried shutting them out mentally by closing my eyes tightly. I tried to calm myself by counting sheep as I lay on my bed, trying desperately to fall asleep. But the sheep I tried to count turned into phantasmagorical dragons and giant elves. They leapt across in the universe dotted with a million stars. They leapt over Jupiter and their hooves made a soothing musical sound that went around in my head. They were the most melodious notes of music I had ever heard. The creatures I saw were a million colours. They were magical, mesmerising and enchanting to look at. With a continuous, carnivsaleque atmosphere inside my head, falling asleep seemed like a remote dream. I was aware of course that it was not 'real' and it existed only in my thoughts but oh, it was so beautiful all the same! It was seductive. I was drawn to it and found myself getting sucked in deeper.

I had always been meticulous about keeping my room tidy. But with so many activities like running, writing poems and studying, I was becoming less sensitive to my surroundings, especially my room. I simply could not be bothered to tidy up and put away stuff when there were a million more interesting things to do. There were piles of books strewn across. There were train tickets and bus tickets lying on the table. There were at least five uncleared, empty coffee mugs. I had no idea how many cups of coffee I had consumed, on the nights that I stayed up writing poetry. The bed was unmade and I could not be bothered to put away the footwear. At least three pairs lay strewn across the floor. There were a few uncleared plates too with residues of food on it, which I had shoved under the bed. My room was increasingly beginning to resemble the chaos that was going on inside my mind. It was a bedlam hotchpotch of a million different things that just existed side by side with no relation or connection to each other, very much like the thoughts racing around inside my head, refusing to stop.

I was becoming increasingly disregardful of my appearance too. I had lost a lot of weight. My already thin frame now looked positively haggard. My eyes took a haunted appearance. Yet they glowed with a kind of energy. But these days I simply could not meet my own eyes in the mirror. As soon as I saw my reflection while brushing my teeth, I would look away hastily, averting my own glance. I hated looking at myself and so I managed with the bare minimum of personal grooming. I simply did not care anymore.

My parents would keep telling me to clean up my room and I would keep promising them that I would do it the next day. Finally my mother could stand it no more and decided to clean it herself, when I was in college.

When I came back one evening, my room was spotless. But there was an uneasy death like silence in the house. One look at my parents' face and I knew something was wrong. My dad's face was as black as storm clouds. My mother was glaring at me angrily, her eyes glowering with rage. I was quite sure that they were angry because I had procrastinated cleaning my room endlessly that they had been forced to do it. I was getting ready to apologise.

That was when I saw it. The letter that Abhi had written to me in blood was laid out on the centre table in the drawing room. Just a glance at it and I felt I had been jabbed hard in the stomach. I sucked in my breath, my heart beating at a furious pace. I swallowed and I opened my mouth and closed it. I did not know what to say. I was speechless. I was shocked that my parents had discovered it. I had never anticipated that. Earlier I had been careful about locking up my cupboard and carrying the key with me when I left home. But lately, I had become careless about that too. Getting a letter like this from a guy and then shamelessly holding on to it, was the ultimate sin a well brought up Indian girl could commit, in their books. To them, it was unforgivable that their daughter whom they trusted so much had done this. One part of me was terrified of their wrath. But another was also numb with the pain of seeing that letter again. It brought back all the memories of the time when I had seen the letter and first gone to his house. It reminded me of the afternoon that I had spent with him, in his house.

"WHAT THE HELL IS THIS?" My dad thundered.

"Is this what we sent you to college for?" My mother added.

"Who is this fellow? And what is this writing in blood? Bloody mad bastard. How dare he?" My dad was so angry that he was choking on his own words. He was shaking with rage. He could hardly speak.

"And have you written back to him, you shameless hussy?" my mom berated me

I did not know what to say. Rage was stirring somewhere in me slowly but there was also a huge wave of sadness brewing. How could my father address him that way? How dare they go though my personal stuff? How could they rob me of my privacy like this and then question me? I was not a child anymore. I was 21 and I could even marry now and they would not be able to stop me.

He is not a mad bastard, dad. He is dead. I wanted to say it but the words stuck somewhere in my throat and did not come out.

My mother looked at me and addressed my dad, "Look at her standing like that. Look at her insolence. She should hang her head in shame. Look at her attitude and her silence. Who the hell does she think she is?"

I still kept quiet. My silence aggravated her anger even more.

"Answer, you shameless whore," she yelled as she shoved me hard. I stepped sideways by the impact of her push. "We did not bring you up for this. Where is this fellow? What is your relationship with him? Are you planning to get married?" she thundered.

My parents were both looking at me now, waiting for me to speak. How could I explain a thing like love to them? Their middle class values, their proper Indian upbringing and everything they stood for, had no place for trivialities like love and romance. If it happened, you pretended it didn't. You brushed it aside and moved on, as life was hard. You studied, you got a job and you got married to the person your parents chose for you. That is what they expected and that is what their way of life was. It was simple and direct. There was no way they would understand passion, love and emotions. There was simply no place for anything like that in their minds or lives.

"He is dead," I finally managed to rasp.

"Very good if he is. He should rot," she said. "Look at her talking back now after doing what she has. This is because you spoilt her and let her get away with everything. We should have been a bit more strict with her. Then we would not have to hear her talking back like this to her own parents," she turned on my dad.

I did not have the courage to explain Abhi's death to them. My mother had presumed I was being discourteous and clammed up when I said that he was dead. I let her think so. It was easier than talking about it.

"Have you ever considered the consequences of keeping this letter?" asked my dad.

I was silent again, standing like a condemned prisoner.

"Is there anything more you have to tell us?" my mother asked.

"No," I said.

"What about these letters then?" she said and that was when I noticed that they had all Vaibhav's letters as well. I had neatly filed them away date wise and the file was now on the sofa in my living room.

I cringed. I was certain they would have read them all as well.

"How many guys will you trap with your wily charms, you stupid little tramp?" My mother almost spat out. Her words cut deep, scooping out my deepest feelings of apprehension and exposing it threadbare.

Till now it had only been a vague feeling of uneasiness inside my head. But by speaking it aloud she had given it a concreteness. I knew she was not entirely correct. It was not as if I had actively pursued or wooed any of these guys. It was they who had pursued me. I had not trapped them in any way. In Abhi's case I had not even told him I loved him. The logical part of me said that I was not responsible in any way. But there was no escape from the *feelings* that I was to blame in some way. Feelings are powerful and logic was crushed under its weight. I was governed by them, not by logic. I was at their mercy and they were unrelenting, harsh and unforgiving.

Unwittingly my mother had struck at the very core of my self esteem and shattered it to pieces. I could not even pick up the bits. Almost immediately I was filled with a deep sense of shame, regret, guilt and hollowness. I felt sick.

"There is only one thing to do now," said my dad. "I want you to promise me that you will stop all this letter writing nonsense. Fortunately, we are far away from Kerala. Nobody should come to know of this. If they do, our family name is gone. We are your parents. We have to think of your future. "

I could not promise my dad anything. I did not even trust myself anymore—what could I promise him? I was silent.

They mistook my silence for acquiescence.

"Come here, there is something we must do," said my dad.

I was too tired even to argue or ask what they had in mind.

I followed my parents to the kitchen balcony.

There was a bottle of kerosene in the corner, along with the household cleaning liquids. My mother generally put a capful of it in the water which the maid used to mop the house. It gave the floors a shine. But that was not what dad had in mind when he took the bottle. I was too dazed to even realise what he was doing.

In almost a flash he had poured some of it on the letters which he had taken out from the file. He threw them on the floor of the balcony. He then struck a match and the flames gobbled up the paper like a hungry monster devouring its prey. It was then that it struck me what he had done. But it was too late now. On top of the pile was Abhi's letter .I watched Abhi's bloodsoaked words going up in flames. The lump in my throat felt like it would explode But I did not cry.

Though I did not shed a single tear, I felt defeated. I had had enough. I wanted to curl up and die. The sense of loss I felt when I saw the letters burn was oppressive. It felt like someone had heated up a hot iron rod and singed me again and again on the raw exposed skin.

"Everything will be fine now. Today onwards you will be a new person. Forget the past. It has gone", my dad had said as I had walked away to my room. He believed it too. He felt I ought to let the past go. After all, I had come to Bombay with a dream to chase and would be armed with a management degree to help me climb the corporate ladder.

But that was not on my mind at that point in time, at all. I went to my room and lay down. I felt empty.

A huge, dark void was inside me now. It was like a phantom pain which amputees experience when a limb is cut off. The limb does not exist anymore but the pain they feel in that limb which no longer exists is very real. I did not know what to do to relieve the pain. I felt trapped in it. I wanted it to stop. I wanted no more of this agony. I curled up my fist as tightly as I could and the finger nails dug deep into the flesh of my palm. I did it again and again. The deeper my nails dug, the better I felt. Then I saw the paper cutting knife which I had bought some time back. I took it and made a small cut on the side of my wrist. I winced slightly as the blade cut the skin and a line of blood appeared. I felt better then. Now at least, the pain was real. I could bear this. It was not like the phantom pain which was terrifyingly unbearable. I made my way to the bathroom and opened the cabinet which had cotton and Dettol. I applied undiluted Dettol directly on the cut. It stung sharply and almost burnt .Oddly, I felt comforted.

My parents had no idea what I had just done. I felt happy that this was one thing they could do nothing about. Their reading of Abhi and Vaibhav's letters had made me feel so violated. This was my body and I could do what I wanted with it. It was a strange kind of defiance. It was a way of getting back at them for what they had done.

"Ha ha Ma, look at me now" I wanted to say. "What are you going to do about this, eh ma?" I wanted to taunt. But fortunately I did nothing of the sort and lay down in my room and counted sleep.

Like before it did not come at all. Earlier I used to be comforted by the phantasmagorical creatures. But they had gone now. They had been replaced by blackness and a void. All I could hear now inside my head were agonising screams of the letters as they burnt. They were cacophonous. Each letter was screaming as it burnt, "save me, save me please let me live". But I was silent as I watched each one dying a slow painful death.

Dad had said that I would be a new person from that day. He had been right but not in a way that he foresaw.

Something inside me had died that day along with those letters. But I did not know what. I could not put a name to it. Perhaps it was a part of my soul. Or maybe it was a part of my destiny.

What it was, I couldn't tell.

15

Deeper down the bottomless pit

I woke up that morning and I remember feeling afraid. It was a kind of fear that I had never known. It was a sinking feeling at the pit of my stomach which was spreading slowly upwards, towards my throat. It felt like somebody had blindfolded me from behind, had his hands around my throat and was squeezing it tight. I felt afraid. Extremely afraid. There was no logical reason to it, really.

I walked to my window on the sixth floor and looked down. Office goers were leaving for work, the children were waiting for their school buses. I peeped into the windows of other apartments and saw women cooking, maids working, children getting ready to leave for school. I looked at the cars that were parked below and the drivers cleaning the cars of their employers. It was a day like any other—an ordinary day.

Except, I was terrified. The fear gripped me. There were no words to express it. It felt overwhelming. My heart was beating fast and I broke into a cold sweat. It was irrational, incomprehensible and terrifying. I wanted to shake it off, but I did not know what to shake off. One part of me tried to rationalise and speak to myself, but it was drowned in the massive panic that I was beginning to experience.

I went back, sat on my bed and took a few deep breaths. I closed my eyes. I put my arms around my feet and rocked back and forth, wanting to calm myself.

"It's okay. It's okay" I kept repeating to myself mentally. But the words seemed to have no effect. I felt fear rising to my throat like bile and could barely breathe.

I did not understand what was happening to me. All I knew was that I was terrified and there was no rationale or logic to it. It was nothing like I had ever experienced before.

I sat on my bed for about fifteen minutes and watched the clock ticking. I felt more and more afraid with each passing second. It felt like I was losing something. I could not put a name to it, but knew it had to be stopped. I felt helpless.

Finally I walked to the kitchen.

I saw my dad making a cup of tea. By now, I could barely breathe.

My face was ashen. My hands were cold.

"Daddy" I called out in a whisper. It was hoarse. My voice could barely be heard. My dad looked up in surprise. One look at me and he knew there was something wrong. Seriously wrong.

"Baby, what is the matter?" He asked. He sounded anxious, tense. He never called me baby before this. At least not that I remembered. It was too much for me to bear. Especially as it sounded so tender and it came after the castigation I had received just the previous evening.

I burst into tears. Uncontrollable sobs. Loud wails initially that gave way to a pitiable whimper. And then silent sobs.

My dad held me "What happened? What happened?" he kept repeating.

I had no idea what happened. Nothing had happened. Nothing that could be explained anyway.

"I am scared, Daddy" I could hear myself say. The voice seemed to belong to somebody else.

"Calm down. Whatever it is we will sort it out." He said.

His words had no effect. By now my mother too had come into the kitchen.

"Is there something wrong at college?" she asked.

There was nothing wrong. Everything at college was indeed fine. I was doing exceedingly well in academics.

I shook my head and I was being entirely truthful, for once. I could not even tell them that I was afraid because the letters were burnt. It was really not because of that. The letters were gone and it was sadness and pain I felt. I had accepted that.

But this was pure fear that I was experiencing.

The fear was rising by the minute. I was in state of panic.

"I am scared, ma. Very scared." I muttered, sounding like a lost child, a six year old.

My emotions were spiralling out of control. It seemed as though I was possessed. I was still sobbing internally.

"What are you scared of? Can you tell?" asked my mother.

I could not.

My parents did not know what to do. They took me to the living room and made me sit on the sofa. My mother me got a bottle of ice cold water and poured out a glass.

"Drink this." she said.

I obeyed. I was breathing fast but had managed to stop sobbing.

Dad was pacing up and down.

"May be it is just taking time for her to adjust to the new course. MBA can be very demanding," said my dad.

"But she has done so well in her first term. Her marks are great. And the other day too at her college fest, she won some contest." retorted my mom.

They were talking as though I wasn't there.

"Is it because of the letters?" My dad asked me.

I shook my head. It really was not.

"Even if we burnt it, we did the right thing. The letters have no place in her life," said my mother.

I did not know what to say. My hands had now turned icy. The soles of my feet felt cold too. My heartbeats had multiplied. It felt like some giant speakers had been attached to them, with an amplifier inside my head and somebody had turned on the volume at full. They seemed to be booming into my ears now. Thud-thud-thud was all I could hear. The room seemed to be closing in on me. I just wanted to sink into the earth and disappear. I did not want to hear anything. I did not want to listen to them discussing about me.

From some place far away, I could hear my mother's voice asking me if I felt better.

I could not respond.

I closed my eyes willing whatever was gripping me to go away. I felt my dad's hand on my back. He was rubbing my back, trying to calm me. He was saying "There is nothing to be afraid of. I am here now. Don't worry. I am here." He kept repeating it and he kept rubbing my back.

I so wanted to believe him.

"Take deep breaths," he said.

I did.

"In and out, Inhale and exhale," he kept repeating. I remember thinking that he was sounding like a yoga instructor on TV and was surprised that even in that state, I could make an association like that.

I breathed just as he had told me and gradually the panic subsided. I began to feel a little better. I opened my eyes.

I saw my mother's worried face. I could see that my dad was worried too but he was trying to hide it.

I felt better now. There was no fear or panic anymore. There was only a very sick feeling—the kind that you get when you have not studied for an exam and you know that the exam is going to start in ten minutes. I was still not completely calm but it was not uncontrollable now. I could think and focus.

Dad and mum could see it on my face.

"What happened?" asked my mom. Her voice was a bit unsteady.

"I don't know, ma." I answered.

"Do you have any exam or test tomorrow?" she asked. Perhaps she thought it was a panic-attack or an anxiety attack. Perhaps she had read about them and had felt that what I had just undergone was a manifestation of stress.

After all, we had just moved to a new town and I had joined a very demanding academic course which would lead to the award of a coveted management qualification, the magic tag that would open corporate doors. It had always been my ambition, like the ambition of most young people those days—to get into a good management institute and then have corporate career , earn big money and to make a career for myself.

What none of us had anticipated was the long nightmare ahead.

My mom thought that it has just been an anxiety attack.

She could not have been more off the mark or more wrong.

Blackness now descended around me like a cloak. I seemed unable to look beyond it. The fear was gone but it was replaced by a depressing feeling which made my heart feel like it weighed a ton. It was a sinking feeling, a feeling that something was just not right, a melancholic, miserable feeling that hung around me now.

I had classes at college the next day and I did not want to go. My parents did not force me.

"You take rest today. Maybe you have been working too hard. You will feel better tomorrow" said my dad, when I told him I did not want to go.

I hoped he was right. I spent the rest of the day in my room, just lying on my bed. I did not feel like reading, I did not feel like making notes, I did not feel like running or writing poetry. Everything that I used to fill my hours with earlier, I did not feel like doing and so I didn't. Perhaps dad was right and maybe I had been driving myself too hard. I decided to try what he suggested.

But the next day too I did not feel any better. Again I stayed at home.

Joseph called up that evening to find out why I had not come to college and my mother picked up the phone. She said I could not come to the phone and I was not well. When I felt better I would come to college and he could speak to me then. She also told him that there was no need to call again. I heard her and now I did not even have the strength to stand up to her. I quietly had accepted her rule of "No boys are allowed to call you on the phone." Even though I was doing a management degree, this rule still seemed to apply. It was archaic but that was my mother. If it was a present day setting, I would probably have received ten text messages from Joseph and my parents wouldn't have been any wiser for it. But in those days, telephones still came with dials and not even push buttons, therefore means of contacting each other were truly limited, unlike today.

In any case I did not feel like speaking to him too. What could I explain? That I stayed at home because I felt an irrational fear and a sinking feeling at the pit of my stomach that refused to go away? It sounded so stupid and so unlike me. It was easier to avoid him and I was too beaten to take anything but the easy way out.

By the fourth day, when I had not gone to college, I knew something was wrong. My parents too sensed it. But none of us were willing to face it. We hoped it would just go away.

On Friday, my dad said "Look Ankita, you are fine physically. Just force yourself to go to college. You will feel better once you meet your friends and do your course work. There is so much you are missing by staying at home. Four days are over now. You listen to me and you go today. Then tomorrow and day-after tomorrow you can again stay home. On Monday you will be fit as a fiddle."

I felt he had a point. So I took my books and left home at the usual time. When I reached the bus stop, the same attack of fear which I had earlier came back. There was again no logical reason for it, just like the last time. Everything outside was just the same as before. This was the same bus-stop that I had caught the bus so many times before. This was where I had come every single day ever since college started. Yet it did not feel like that today. I tried rationalising with myself saying nothing had changed. But logic and rationalisation had no place inside my head like before. The traffic, people and other things around me were going about their usually business, just like before. But for me, the world seemed to have stopped. I was paralysed with fright.

I broke into a cold sweat. My palm went cold and again I could not breathe. I sat for ten minutes in the bus stop trying to get my mind into some kind of order. The other passengers around me were blissfully unaware of my inner turmoil. Everything was normal for them and it was just another ordinary day. But to me, it felt like the end of the world. Finally, in a daze I made my way home, somehow. My mother opened the door to my frantic ringing of the doorbell.

"What happened? Are you all right? She asked, worry writ large over her face. My dad had already left for work. My mother looked anxious. She wanted me to assure her that I was fine.

I could not.

I was not fine.

It was the first time I realised that there was perhaps something very wrong. I had hoped badly that whatever it was would become fine when I went to college.

"Look Ankita. Just be strong. These are simply thoughts inside your head. You can just snap out of it by controlling your thoughts," said my mother.

Oh how I tried! I wanted to snap myself out of it. I willed it to go away. I tried thinking of happy things. I tried calling back my giant creatures and elves with musical hooves. They refused to come to my aid. All that was left now was a huge void and blackness.

When my dad came home from work, I overheard my mother telling him what had happened that morning. Dad came to my room immediately and tried talking to me. He asked me how I was.

I felt I had let him down in some way. I started crying. I could not seem to stop the tears.

My parents did not know it at that time and neither did I that it was something much larger than any of us had envisaged, anticipated or foreseen.

It was the beginning of a sharp curve, a painful detour, a journey that would lead me completely away from my destination, to the edge of a cliff. A journey that would almost take my life, destroy me completely, suck the life force out of me and then toss me away as an empty shell.

And the worst part was that it had just begun.

16

The ink blots

When I shifted to Bombay with dreams in my eyes and hopes in my heart, trampling over love and other such trivial things that young boys and girls of that age normally indulged in, the last thing I had anticipated or foreseen was finding myself at the door of a psychiatrist's clinic.

I had tried to fool myself and fool my parents as well, assuring them that I was fine. I had told them I would be okay in a few days. They had believed me. I too had believed myself. After all, it was indeed just what I felt and it was all in my head. I thought I would be very strong and shake it off. I tried my best to force myself. But things only got worse.

I stayed at home for a week more and by then it was clear to me that I was not in any position to go back to my course. I did not tell my parents what I had realised. Unknown to them, the same panic attacks that came earlier had happened two more times, when I had tried to think about going back to my college. So I pushed it aside and refused to think about it. I did not want these terrifying attacks to come back. My parents did not know what to do. They were at their wits end. When they asked me when I would resume my studies, I told them to give me just a few days more.

My father called up the college and spoke to the Dean. I don't know what he told them. I did not want to know. It was like I wanted to shut out college and anything to do with it.

The blackness was now a permanent thing. It surrounded me all the time, refusing to go away. The void was a permanent feature. It was like I was dead from inside. Earlier I had been experiencing a deep sense of pain. But now it seemed to have been replaced by a bottomless pit. I was totally the opposite of what I had been a few weeks back. I did not feel any inclination to run. I felt no interest in my management books. I felt no interest in anything. I just wanted to lie in my bed and go deeper into the vacuum which was now my mind. I looked at the poems I had written earlier. I tried to make myself feel some passion, to stir in myself some kind of feeling, to push myself to be what I used to be. But I failed. Miserably. No words came. No thoughts came. It was a horrible place to be trapped in. I did not want to be there. But there seemed to be no escape.

The last straw came when I tried to read. I picked up a book which lay on my table, which I had bought, a long time back, while I was in Cochin, intending to read it. It was Arthur Hailey's *Hotel.* I opened it and tried to read it. It gave me a rude jolt. I was shocked to discover that by the time I reached the end of a sentence I could not remember what was at the beginning. I tried again. Then once more. And yet again. I just could not believe it. Along with my words, I seemed to have lost the ability to read and comprehend too.

I tried telling myself that it was because I was distracted and I could of course read. I had devoured so many books, that too far heavier than this. Besides, this was something I would enjoy reading too. No matter what I did or how hard I tried, I just could not do it. The more I tried, the more I failed.

Then, I opened my file of coloured coded notes that I had so meticulously made. I tried reading them. I could not read even beyond a paragraph. I had no idea what they meant. I would read the same sentence over and over without comprehending a single thing. It was as though my mind could focus only on one word for a very brief period, perhaps a few seconds and the next second, it had forgotten it. The words vanished from my mind like the chalk writings on a blackboard being wiped clean. I seemed to no longer have any control over them. Then I opened the Kotler book and a feeling of nausea flooded me. I looked at the marketing jargon and felt sick. The sinking feeling which was now a permanent fixture rose higher, drowning me. Frustration, rage, tears and helplessness welled up inside me. I closed my fingers again and my nails dug deep.

I tried one more time. It was simply no use. It was like somebody had switched off some important part of my brain which controlled reading, comprehension and even thinking. I felt like a broken toy. I felt a deep sense of hopelessness. The helplessness of the situation that I found myself in was too much to bear. I did not know what to do. Life, as I knew it, had vanished, handing me in its place this mockery to make sense of. Everything I had taken for granted had disappeared. It was simply unbearable. In a fit of pure frustration, I swept the file containing my notes, the Kotler book and a few other sheets of paper off my desk.

They went crashing to the floor along with a reading lamp that the book hit while being swept off. The bulb of the lamp broke and I felt like it was my life. My parents came running into the room hearing the noise.

"What happened?" asked my mother.

"Are you all right, Ankita?" asked my dad.

I was too ashamed to admit that I had pushed the things on to the floor. I knew there was no way I could explain to my parents that I was not able to read, rather comprehend what I was reading anymore. I myself could not understand it. Then how could I expect my parents to? What could I tell them about this scary new thing that I had just discovered? It would only worry them more. As it is, they were so anxious about me. Even now as they spoke, I could see the worry and the anxiety written all over their faces.

"The lamp slipped while I was tidying up," I lied.

"You should be more careful. Look now the glass pieces have spread all over," said my mom.

I didn't say anything and I began picking up the pieces. My parents believed what I had said and left me alone.

After they went I felt as though the room was closing in on me.

I feel down and depressed. I feel worthless. I don't know what is happening to me and why I am feeling this way. There is really no reason. I have tried to make these thoughts go away. I have failed. I don't want to do this MBA anymore. I can't bear the thought of looking at Joseph, Chaya and Jigna again. The thought of seeing my classmates faces make me sick. The professors, the course material, the case studies—I just do not want to set my eyes on them again. I don't want to tell all this to my parents either. They have high hopes about me. They are so proud of me and if I drop out, they really will have no face to show the people to whom they so proudly boasted of my achievements.

My throat feels dry. I sit with my head in my hands. For how many hours I sit like this I don't know. I feel I cannot go on anymore. There is nothing left to live for. There is nothing to look forward to. I pick up a pen and try to write what I am feeling. But words too seem to have abandoned me. Nothing comes. I am unable to write too. Just like I am unable to read. I scribble on the paper hard. Round and round, round and round, I scribble and press hard with the tip of the pen until the paper tears. Then I cast it aside and I continue sitting still, staring into the blank.

This is frightening, this world without words, this world of darkness and void. I don't want to be here anymore. I want to make it stop.

I remember the paper cutting knife again. I take it and this time I want to hurt myself really bad. I want to kill this pain inside me which refuses to go away. I want to feel better. I want to give this pain a physical form.

I must have walked into the bathroom with the knife.

The next thing I remember is my dad trying to grab it from me. I resisted with all my might and I swung my right hand which had the knife, trying to push him away with my left. The knife made a cut all across my left forearm, extending from the back of the arm, almost at the centre, running diagonally across it, ending just near the wrist. The sight of blood shocked my mother who had come rushing out of her bedroom, hearing the commotion.

"WHAT IN THE WORLD WERE YOU TRYING TO DO?" screamed my dad. There was shock, pain and grief in his voice.

"Oh my God, Oh My God. What has happened to her?" repeated my mother over and over again. She was crying.

I was unmoved. Strangely I was feeling a little relieved that the focus of the pain could now be shifted to elsewhere. My dad applied the astringent to the cut on my arm and covered the cut with cotton. He tied a crepe bandage around it to make the blood stop.

I never felt more alone that night as I lay on my bed, sleep still evading me. My parents would not leave me alone after that. They took turns watching me. They did it out of concern. They were genuinely worried. But I felt like a prisoner. I felt trapped and frightened. I did not want to be watched over like this. This way I felt, it was becoming difficult to breathe. I did not even want to eat, but my parents forced me to. I would eat just to satisfy them, the bare minimum that my body could manage with. I wanted everything to just end. I did not want to be in this situation anymore. I was tired. I was defeated. I was broken too.

Finally on the fourth night I promised them I would never ever do it again. My dad wanted me to agree to accompany him to the psychiatrist. I was too beaten to even argue and that was how I found myself that morning, outside the clinic, wearing a full sleeved shirt to hide the scar on my left arm.

I felt like a sacrificial lamb waiting to be executed. I hated the look of the building itself. The clinic was on the ground floor of a three storied building, which seemed to need a coat of paint badly. Dad had made an appointment and my mother too had accompanied us.

The doctor was a woman called Mukta Nagraj who looked very

young. She wore a saree and her short hair was neatly styled. She seemed to take great pride in her numerous academic qualifications as the wall behind her was decorated with various medical degrees from various colleges all over the world. I was least interested in meeting her. I was doing this only for my parents' sake.

"Hello, Good morning. You must be Ankita" she greeted me glancing at the list of appointments she had in her diary which was open at her desk.

I did not respond. Her manner was fake, her smile was professional and it appeared as though she was genuinely concerned. But I could see through it. I hated the sight of her. My dad explained to her that we had recently moved from Cochin. He explained how I had got into one of the most coveted management schools in Bombay. He told her about how bright I was academically, how I had won the elections. Then he explained how I was doing well academically in the Management course too but how I was now reluctant to go back. I was grateful that he did not mention the incident with the knife.

She listened carefully and then told my parents that she wanted to speak to me in private. They said they would wait outside.

She looked at me and smiled again.

I looked at her sullenly.

"Can you answer a few questions for me Ankita?"

I want to hit you so hard that the stupid smirk on your face vanishes forever.

"Yes."

"Have you been sleeping well lately?"

What concern is that of yours, bitch?

"Not as well as before."

She quizzed me endlessly. Had I been eating well? Had I enjoyed the course? What other things was I interested in? How did I feel about the move? Did I miss my old life? If I had a chance to go back to Cochin, would I like to? What did I feel about travelling in trains in Bombay? Was it a huge change to shift from a small place to a big town?

I answered in monosyllables. I was angry about my life being pried open like this.

Then she asked me something which I had no monosyllabic answer for.

"If you don't mind, could you tell me if you were romantically involved with someone?"

One is dead, one is madly in love with me and one would be wondering right now what is happening and why he isn't able to get in touch with me and would be desperate to talk to me.

"No," I lied. There was no way I was telling this smirking condescending woman my life story. What would she do? Advise me and everything would be all right? I would feel instantly better and go back to my course?

She did not advise me at all. She did something worse. She asked if I was okay with taking a few psychological tests. She said it would help her in her analysis. I thought of refusing. Then I thought of my parents waiting outside with hope and anxiety. So I agreed.

"Okay," she said. "I am going to show you a few images and I want you to tell me what you associate with them as soon as you see them. Just don't think too much about them. Just tell me what you feel they could be as soon as you see them. I will be writing down whatever you say. These are for my notes. Don't bother about that." She said

I nodded.

She smiled again.

Hatred oozed out of my pores like molten lava but I concealed it. I just could not bring myself to smile back at her smug, superior self though.

She took out the first card, which was about the size of an A4 paper. It had an ink blot on it, a very abstract black and white ink-blot and showed it to me. She asked me what I saw.

I could see at least fifty things in it depending on which way was up and which way you looked at it.

"What way is it placed?" I asked.

"Anyway dear, just tell me what you see!" she could not keep the condescending tone out of her voice.

It took all my self control not to snatch the card out of her hand and hit her repeatedly across her face with it.

I looked at the card instead and immediately told her at least ten things I could see. She wrote them all down. I asked her if she wanted me to tell her more. I was sure this time I could not keep the superior tone out of *my* voice. I felt quite proud of my creative abilities and visual skills.

She said that was enough.

I smiled for the first time in days.

Then she continued this exercise with more cards. There were ten in all. I was beginning to enjoy it.

Then it was all over.

She told me to give her 5 minutes while she studied my responses.

She took about twelve minutes.

Then she called my parents in.

"I have studied her responses, and analysed what she has told me in depth. I have also analysed the test which she just did."

My parents nodded gratefully eager for anything she would say, waiting for whatever little scraps of her wisdom which would shed some light on why their daughter, their star child was behaving like this.

"She has severe depression. We should start her on medication immediately. That will help her a lot. Otherwise her condition will worsen," she pronounced.

Then she wrote out a prescription with names of some tablets I had never heard of, before.

My parents took it from her hands like it was a gem.

"These will just help her sleep better and also regulate her low mood," she said.

She asked my parents to come back with me after two weeks when she would assess me again and adjust dosage if needed. Then we were dismissed and I saw her already glancing at her next appointment.

I wondered how much my parents had paid for this. I wondered how much this lady made in a day. It must have been a huge packet, judging by the number of patients that were waiting, whom I noticed on the way out. We must have been her first appointment for the day.

My dad stopped off at a Chemist's shop and bought the tablets she had prescribed.

"Don't worry Ankita," he said as he entered the car. "Everything will be just fine. You will be okay soon." The hope in his voice broke my heart.

That was when I started crying.

I couldn't stop even when we reached home.

17

The light goes out

I got progressively worse. The medication which the doctor had prescribed did not seem to help the least bit. My parents were convinced it would work and a cure was just round the corner. Sadly it was like the elusive lottery that hopefuls keep buying week after week, in anticipation of a jackpot. But they were as unaware of failure as I was.

The tablets were to be taken twice a day. There was a little yellow one and a slightly larger white one. I had no idea what they were for and what they were called. But my parents had pinned their hopes and their aspirations for me on these two little tablets which held the promise of miraculously, or rather medically, turning my life around.

Each morning my dad stood at the foot of my bed with the tablets in hand and a glass of water. Almost every day, the same story repeated itself.

"Dad, I really do not want to take these. They make me drowsy," I would say.

"Ankita, your body and mind both need rest. If you don't take the medicine how will you get better? This is only temporary. Now be a good girl and take it," he would coax patiently.

I would then swallow both at once and he would be pleased.

I felt a little bit like a prisoner but the only place that I was trapped in, was inside my own mind. The worst thing was that there was no escape.

The medication made me drowsy. I slept when I felt like and woke up when I felt like it. What was truly terrifying was the blankness. There were simply *no thoughts* inside my head. It was all a blank. It was an endless vacuum, a huge void. Earlier, I had sought refuge in the magnificent images that I could conjure up without an effort. I could write what I felt. I could pour my emotions and my feelings into words. I had my poetry and my pictures and words. But this terrible and completely strange state that I found myself in, was something that I just could not bear. The agony of it made me want to weep and wail out my sorrow but even grief eluded me. I was numb and senseless. I ached to feel something. I ached to feel pain. I ached to cry. I ached to think. I ached and ached. The ache was a constant companion like a shadow. There was no getting rid of it. It never went away and the moment I opened my eyes, it was there, prodding me, hurting me, taunting me and mocking me. I wanted to run away from it. I wanted a respite. I wanted to escape. I just wanted to be able to *feel* once more.

Nights and days merged into one another. I could not bear the light and would draw the curtains of my room and shut the windows. If my parents as much as tried to open it even a teeny bit, I would scream asking them to let it be. I was beginning to develop an affinity towards anything that was dark. During the waking hours, it was pure agony to just remain alive. The pain was terrifying. Everything that was once attractive and interesting now appeared drab. What had come easily at one point in time took a massive effort now. It was a huge ordeal to even wake up and get out of bed. I preferred lying in the dark, with the darkness of my mind and the blankness for company. I wanted to be left alone. If my parents tried to sit with me, I would get agitated and angry and tell them to go away and let me be in peace. They did not know what to do and hence most of the time, left me alone, only coming in to see that I had my tablets.

I looked at the books arranged neatly on my desk and felt sick. Whether it was the medication or my state of mind, I do not know, but I went to the toilet and threw up violently. I had no idea of the time of the day. It was always dark in my room, anyway. I sat for what seemed like hours next to the toilet bowl, throwing up every now and then. Finally too exhausted even to stand, I curled up and slept on the bathroom floor. I must have been a sight with dishevelled hair, blood shot eyes and dried vomit caking my mouth. A bit of it on was on my clothes too. I was woken up by my mother.

"Oh God! Get up, get up," she was shaking me, holding my shoulders. "How long have you been lying here?"

I opened my eyes with a great effort. The light stung them and I scrunched up my eyes to avoid the shaft of light that was piercing them like sharp needles. I had no idea of time. I had probably slept the whole night on the bathroom floor. I felt sicker than even before. But my stomach was empty and there was nothing more I could throw up. The bitter retching continued to wrack my body even as I tried to control it.

"Wash your face and rinse your mouth, you will feel better," said my mother.

I did as I was told and went and lay down in my room again.

I felt completely useless. Even little things seemed impossible to do now. I felt stupid, dumb and totally inadequate. All I seemed to be able to do was to lie in my bed from morning to night. It was the only thing that I was capable of doing. It was as though the light that was inside me had gone out. It was a dark hole and I had no idea when it would end. St. Agnes and everything that had happened there seemed a distant dream. Even my getting admission into a management institute seemed like something that had happened to someone else. I did not feel like the same person anymore. I could not come to terms with it.

To be trapped like this in one's own body is a fate worse than death. With death, at least there is an end. Here the suffering is endless. You cannot run from yourself. The torment is bestial. I constantly felt as though somebody was tearing out my heart from the ribcage, severing the arteries, yanking it out, tossing it aside and then stomping over it, squelching it under heavy feet. All I could do was watch helplessly. I felt this day in and day out. Every waking hour was a cruel reminder of what I had once been. I was in a worse state than before and my parents took me back to see Dr. Mukta. I accompanied them without a fuss. She wanted to talk to me alone, like before.

Looking at her now, I felt frightened. I felt like a rat that they use in scientific experiments. The rage I felt towards her earlier was now replaced by naked fear. My hands were trembling when I faced her. They were cold and I clutched them hard, rolling my palms into a fist. I felt like an injured animal and wanted to hide in the safety and darkness of my room. Here in her clinic, with her cold eyes studying my every move, I felt disrobed and vulnerable. I wanted to scream but I was too terrified to even let out a whimper.

"And how are we now Ankita?" she asked brightly in her falsetto professional voice.

I could not answer.

"Medicines working well?" she asked. I felt like there was mockery too in her tone.

I clenched my fists tighter. My heartbeats increased. There was cold sweat beginning to trickle down my armpits, beneath my clothes. I could not meet her eyes. I looked down and looked away.

Finally, perhaps tired of my unresponsiveness, she called my parents in.

"It may seem as though the medicines are not taking effect, but trust me, this is how is supposed to proceed," she said.

These were the words my parents wanted to hear.

"She is sleeping better than before and the restlessness is so much under control," she said.

But I feel dead inside. Don't you realise you are killing me bit by bit?

My parents nodded eagerly, lapping up every word, taking comfort in her assurances.

"There is one more medicine I would like to introduce her to, this week. It will help her mind to focus as it will bring her serotonin levels back to normal" she said smoothly and wrote out a new prescription with a practised flourish.

"Is this in addition to the ones she is taking?" asked my dad.

"Yes," she replied. The one she is taking is just a mild relaxant which was to calm her down. This is the real treatment. You will see the difference. I will see you after two more weeks."

I was totally helpless. I did not want more medication. I wanted my poems back. I wanted my pictures back. They were the only hope I had and they had vanished. But I had no choice in the matter.

The new medicine left a strange kind of dryness in my throat that seemed to be perpetually scratching it from inside. It made me very uncomfortable. I felt an odd kind of restlessness. I felt like throwing up all the time, but it was only retching and nothing came out. When I slept I suddenly woke up in cold sweat, breathing hard. It felt like I had been pushed into a living hell.

I sat at my desk staring at my books. I looked at the Kotler book which was on top of the pile of books neatly arranged. At one time I had revelled in its contents greedily devouring it. I opened it yet again hoping to be comforted by familiar words and phrases. I felt that the earlier inability to read and absorb would now have vanished and it would all come back easily to me. I was wrong. When I opened it and tried to read, frustration, panic and rage gripped me once again. It was just the same as before. Nothing had changed. In blind anger I once again grabbed the reading light and sent it flying across the room. I threw the Kotler book too against the wall and it fell with a heavy thud. Then I smashed the ceramic cup that had pens and pencils on to the ground. The cup shattered and the pens scattered in all directions. Then in a fury I began tearing up the notes I had meticulously made. I was breathing hard and there were tears running down my face. The commotion made my parents come running.

I stopped dead in my tracks when I realised that they were watching me in shock, not knowing what to do. Girls expressing rage like this was not something that was easily accepted in Indian society. They did not know what to do or how to deal with it. I too was slightly shocked with my violent reaction.

Later when I went to the bathroom, I happened to catch site of my full length reflection and got a jolt. Gone was the pencil thin me. I did not recognise the apparition that was giving me a startled look from the mirror. I had gained so much weight in all the time that I had stayed home, just lying in bed. In place of my eyes were frightened slits that gazed back at me. My cheeks were puffed up. I had even developed a pot belly. My hair was dishevelled and knotty. I did not remember when I had combed it last. My skin had taken on an unhealthy shade of pale yellow like someone afflicted with jaundice.

My ordeals were far from over. I had to meet Dr. Mukta again the following week with my parents. She then said to continue with the same medication but adjusted the dosage and made it a higher dose.

It was the proverbial last straw that broke the camel's back. I was already broken but this crushed me completely and totally.

The biggest irony was that everybody felt that I was indeed getting better and would soon resume my classes. But nobody had a clue as to what was really happening.

On the outside, I looked like death.

And inside, I felt like it.

I was tired of it all. I wanted it to end. There was only one way out of this misery. It was my only escape.

Quietly but determinedly I made up my mind to take my own life.

18

A plan for a final exit

It was after nine more weeks of misery, hopelessness and excruciating agony that I finally gathered enough courage and attempted to kill myself the second time.

My parents eventually figured out that Dr. Mukta's medication had not been effective and I had shown no signs of improving. They dragged me to a second psychiatrist, supposedly one of the best in the whole country. He made Dr. Mukta seem like an angel.

Appointments had to be made weeks in advance. He was one of the busiest psychiatrists in the country, I was told. My parents considered it fortunate that he had agreed to examine me. I felt no gratitude, no happiness. I was numb with pain and the senselessness of it. I was silent and refused to speak to either of my parents. When they asked me to accompany them, I went along quietly.

His clinic was tiny and despite being on time for the appointment, we had to wait for nearly an hour and forty minutes before he could see us. The tiny waiting room was cramped with a whole lot of people. I averted their eyes and looked down at my feet as we waited. Dr. Kohli was bald, over weight and had a French beard. He seemed to be a smoker too judging by the stench of tobacco in his little cabin, where he examined patient's day in and day out.

He did not even speak to me and merely wrote out prescription for more medication. He spoke to my parents as though I did not exist. Dr. Mukta had at least made an effort, however professional it was, to at least attempt to find out how I was feeling. Dr. Kohli seemed to think that such niceties were a waste of time especially when he had hundreds of patients clamouring for his attention, jostling for space in that tiny clinic on the third floor of an old building with narrow derelict stairs, in a crowded Bombay suburb.

Increasingly, as each day passed, I was convinced about the futility of my existence. I felt a mounting sense of despair not only about my inability to do anything remotely useful but also about the stress and strain I was putting my parents through. They still believed I would get better and refused to give up on me. They saw to it that I took the medication that Dr. Kohli had prescribed diligently. What he drugged me with, seemed to me thrice the amount that Dr. Mukta had given. I was perpetually like a zombie and had settled down into my new persona with ease. I was too tired to fight, too tired to argue and too tired to protest. It was as though I had accepted that this was my fate.

I began avoiding all human contact. I did not want to run into anybody from my residential complex. I did not want to make conversation with anybody or explain why I was not going to college anymore to anyone. I lived in constant terror of meeting people and facing people. I did not want anyone to see me in this state. I was overweight, ugly and drab. I was no longer what I used to be and could not stand myself. My sense of humour and my quick wit had vanished completely. I could not even make small conversation anymore. I was a burden not only on my parents but also on my own self. My existence was completely pointless. There was only one way out of this mess and that was to end my own life.

I had been contemplating various methods of suicide quite clinically. I had thought about it for weeks. I thought of slashing my wrists and then submerging them in a bucket of water which would ensure that I bled to death. In the movies, they usually do it in bathtubs. But our bathroom had no bath tub and the closest I could think of was a bucket of water which would do the trick. There were two reasons why I decided against this method. It would be messy the next day and also this was a slow method. I was not sure if I would have that much of sustenance as to hold my hands under the water all the time till life ebbed out. The other method I considered was pouring kerosene all over myself and getting burnt like the letters. But here too what terrified me was the chance of failure. I had seen photographs of people with third degree burns. If I failed, the suffering would be unimaginable. I would get cooked from the inside. Also there was a risk of permanent disfigurement. Then I thought of hanging from the ceiling fan which was the most common method used in movies. I could easily use my mother's *saree* which was what they did in the movies. But I was not sure if I would be able to make the loop correctly. Besides I was not sure if I could go through with it. It involved too many parameters all of which had to work for it to be successful. Then I also contemplated on an overdose of my medication. I knew that my medication was kept on top of the refrigerator and all I had to do was swallow them all and then lie down in my bed and go. This one appealed to me but I was not sure if the tablets would be lethal enough. I was not sure of what effect it would have. I also was not sure whether my body could take it all or whether I would throw it up. So I ruled out this option too. Finally the only one which seemed most likely to work was jumping off the terrace of the building I lived in. Death would be certain and quick. I winced only for a moment when I pictured my body hitting the hard concrete, the momentum and impact that would crush my bones and perhaps my skull and make my heart cease working. I was sure that I would feel the pain only for a few seconds. I had read that if one were to fall from a height of fifty feet it would be lethal. I would be jumping off the eighth floor –therefore I could be certain of death.

It must have been around eleven, in the night when I crept out quietly.

I went up to the terrace of my building. Usually it was not locked as the maintenance people went to the terrace often for fixing Television antennas, and tending to other problems like water tanks and plumbing lines. I went out to the terrace. The cold night air hit me. I took in a deep breath.

I looked at the night sky with a million twinkling stars. I remembered my night at the fresher's party on another terrace in Bombay where I was teasing Joseph, threatening to jump off. The irony of the situation struck me now. There was no Joseph now to tease and I only wanted to die now.

I went to the edge of the wall of the terrace and looked down. The hard concrete pavement eight floors below stared at me, as if daring me to jump. The cars were parked in neat rows in pre designated parking slots. Beside them I could see the tree tops. I peered a little further, and walked along the edge of the wall, choosing a spot to jump. I did not want to land in anyone's balcony. I had to pick a spot where there were no balconies or no saving spaces of any kind underneath. The best spot was where the toilets were located. There were only plumbing lines here that ran along the height of the wall.

I stood at the spot and stared down. The night was eerily silent. Not a leaf stirred. Usually the night watchman made his rounds around the building but I knew from my sleepless nights, that he would begin his rounds only past midnight. I would be dead and gone by then.

I climbed on the wall and sat looking down, gathering those final moments in my head.

It was then that I heard the hushed voices.

"Oh Keerti, I really love you. All I am asking you to do is just think about what I have said" said a male voice.

In my already confused head, it sounded to me exactly like Abhi's voice and it was very similar to what Abhi had said to me. Stunned I turned around.

It was Sanchit, along with a girl. I remembered having met them when I had first moved to Bombay. Both lived in my building. They had taken shelter just next to the water tank. Sanchit's back was turned towards me. Keerti was facing him.

Abhi's grandfather's words came back again to haunt me "Never belittle love," he had said.

I was distracted and I continued staring at them transfixed.

"Ankita. Oh my God. What in the world are you doing here?" Suddenly my dad's voice cut through my thoughts and the next moment I turned around and saw my dad.

My dad's voice had alerted Sanchit and Keerti too, and I saw them moving away quietly to the other side of the building making their way behind the water tanks. I don't think they were aware that I had already spotted them.

My dad was shocked. He had woken up with an uneasy feeling that night, and when he came to my room, he had found it empty. It was almost as though he had a premonition or maybe he had heard me when I had gone out of the door. He had then found the entrance door to our flat unlocked and had gone downstairs and asked the security guard if he had seen me. When the Guard had answered in the negative, my dad had come up to the terrace to look for me.

I did not know what to say to him. But I am sure that he had understood my intentions perfectly looking at my passive face and crumpled, defeated shoulders.

I had never seen my dad cry, but that night I saw the tears of defeat and agony that he blinked back. I saw the sheer helplessness and anger at being able to do nothing for me on his face. He was such a strong man, a self made man who had risen from the starkest of circumstances to carve out a life and a career for himself. He had always given us the best of everything.

But that night, I saw him break and it was because of me.

He did not say a word to me. He did not shout at me or berate me. I wished he had. His words would have been easier to bear than his silence. He took my hands in his and quietly led me down the stairs back intc out apartment on the second floor.

"Sorry Pa," I managed to finally say, choking on my own words. It was the hardest apology I have ever made in my life.

I truly meant it.

But I had no more words left to convey its depth.

19

No way out

I wait my turn on the chair outside the doctor's office. The psychiatrist, to be precise. The so-called expert. We have travelled all the way from Bombay to Bangalore to make this trip. Getting an appointment here is like getting an appointment to meet the Pope at the Vatican City. It is one of the best mental health care centres in India.

The nurse calls out my patient number. No one cares about my name or what I used to be. I rise to enter his office.

Then he starts asking the questions. I hate someone prying into my life like this. I hate having to go through all this.

I feel trapped, cornered, exasperated and suddenly very tired. I just want it to end.

So I start to answer.

The questions were exactly like the ones Dr. Mukta had asked me before. But this was a lot more in detail. Not only was he asking the questions which were detailed and precise, he was also recording my responses. He was writing down everything I was saying.

He took his time recording all my answers. He then asked me to wait outside while he would discuss with the senior doctors, Dr. Shah and Dr. Madhusudan. He said they would want to speak to my parents.

I went outside, sent my parents in, and settled down on the cold metallic chair in the waiting hall. It was large and there were at least a hundred patients and their relatives. How it was possible that so many people had mental health problems? How could so many people need help like this? Were they also depressed like me? What issues did they have? I wondered if there were any management school drop outs like me. I doubted it.

It was after about fifteen whole minutes that my parents emerged. Their faces were grim.

"Ankita, the senior doctors here have discussed your case. They feel that it is best that you are admitted and kept under observation," said my dad, as he put his hand on my shoulder.

It sounded to me like a death sentence. I was in complete shock. I did not want to come here in the first place. Now they were going to keep me here. It was so unacceptable to me. But they were not giving me any choice.

I could not speak even though I wanted to scream.

"We have opted for a private room for you. It is the best they have. You will get better very soon," my dad continued.

"Please dad, take me back home. I promise I will not do anything like that again," I pleaded with him. I felt disgusted with myself for pleading this way with my parents. But the dread and fear of being admitted at a mental hospital made me overcome my reluctance and

I pleaded again.

"Please dad, please don't leave me here," I said again.

"Look, this is not easy for us," he said. "But this is for the best. How long can we go on like this? You were not getting any better. We have already tried two psychiatrists. This is the best medical care in the country. You will be looked after well here," he said with finality in his voice.

I closed my eyes and tried to calm my pounding heartbeats. I desperately looked around my surroundings.

I was now trapped not only mentally but physically as well in this place, which promised a cure.

More than ever, I wanted to die, but there was now no way out even for death.

It was only after my parents went out and left me alone with the attendant, in the private room which they had selected for me, that the now familiar sensation of fear and panic began setting in, like an old and dear friend who turns up uninvited to your home at an inconvenient time.

The room was nondescript. It was like any normal hospital room in a Government run hospital. A high bed made of iron, painted white, the bumpy rust beginning to show around the corners, dirty green industrial paint on the walls that was beginning to peel, a door that led to a bathroom with mosaic tiles that had seen better days and the unmistakable smell of disinfectant which all hospitals reek of. Years later, the smell would haunt me and would still have the power to send me into panic but I did not know that then. All I felt was a gnawing sense of abandonment which engulfed me, dragging me down. I, a full grown adult, felt like a two year old child that cries out for its mother, when she vanishes. I hated myself. I did not want to admit that I needed my parents. I wanted to be strong. I wanted to be in control. I did not want to be here, alone, all by myself in the ward of a mental hospital, relegated as a patient, a highly disturbed one at that, needing high observation and care.

But the fear was coming back. I began to experience the now familiar sinking feeling of panic in the pit of my stomach which was slowly spreading upwards. I needed them. I wanted them to stay. I wanted my mother to hug me and tell me that she was here for me. I wanted her to say that I mattered to her. I wanted her to comfort me and reassure me that things were going to be fine.

She did nothing of the sort.

"Ma, dad. Please don't go. Please," I called out, pleading, in a tone that I myself did not recognise, a tone that sounded alien to my own ears.

I could see my mother turning away with lips pursed, covering her mouth with a handkerchief and my father steadying her, his hand around her shoulder as they walked out.

I was filled with a deep sense of rage, helplessness, frustration, anger and a sinking feeling of abandonment. How could they leave me like this? How could they agree to let me be admitted in a mental hospital? I wasn't crazy. I didn't want to be here.

At that moment I hated the world. I hated my parents. I hated life. I hated everything. I was filled with a loathing so dark, so deep and so impenetrable that it was hard to see anything else. All that was going on inside my head was that I was now admitted in a mental hospital and I was alone.

"I HATE YOU. BOTH OF YOU.COME BACK HERE—

DON'T LEAVE ME LIKE THIS—YOU'RE MY PARENTS DAMMIT." I did not realise that I was screaming at the top of my voice. I did not even notice that I was trembling with rage, clenching my fists and yelling.

"WHY THE FUCK DID YOU GIVE BIRTH TO ME? COME BACK DAMMIT—COME BACK," I continued yelling. I knew vaguely that I was losing control, but my emotions were ruling me completely. I looked around for something to throw at the door, but could see nothing. I clenched the stark white sheets instead and yanked them off the bed. The pillow went flying out, with the force.

The doctor would later write in my case history sheet "Patient hysterical. Sedative administered."

I could see the nurse coming running in with two more attendants.

"She is out of control," the Nurse said to attendant next to her.

"SHUT UP," I yelled at her. "What the fuck do you know about out of control?" I turned my rage on her, my voice hysterical which again I did not recognise.

She wasn't listening.

It was then that I saw the syringe in her hand. Both the attendants were now on either side of me and held my arms down. The rage that had risen like industrial smoke out of a giant furnace was threatening to blind me now. I wanted to smash their heads in. How dare they decide that I was out of control? I was furious. Who were they to deny me the expression of my anger? I kicked out with one leg, but the nurse had already driven the syringe in. I felt humiliated, insulted and helpless. So deep were my emotions that I was shaking and couldn't talk anymore.

I broke down into loud sobs and settled on the bed. I don't

remember much as the sedative they had injected was beginning to take effect and my eyes shut.

When I recovered consciousness, all I felt was an incredible sense of calmness. There was a dull pain in my jaw and I had a very slight headache. My throat was parched, as if I had not drunk water in a year. But the panic was gone, so was the rage. For a few minutes I could not recall where I was and what had happened to me. I was a little confused. It seemed like a dream. Had I fallen down? What was this strange green colour that I was seeing? Which room in my home had this colour? I could not recall any room having these walls.

Then it began sinking in slowly. I was in hospital. 'mental hospital' a voice inside my head reminded me, taunting me and I winced, feeling a deep sense of shame. The ever popular, much adored, outgoing, smart, bright, promising young star of St. Agnes was now a patient in a mental hospital.

"Hello Ankita. I'm Sister Rosaline. How are you feeling? Do you want some water?" asked a nurse.

"Hello Sister. Yes please and sorry about the yelling earlier," I said. I felt genuinely ashamed now at losing control like that and yelling at her. I noticed her now. She seemed to have kind eyes. She was pleasantly plump, must be in her fifties and seemed to be very experienced.

"Oh, that is perfectly okay, child," She said smiling as she handed me a bottle of water.

As I drank thirstily, she added "Patients generally respond well to ECT."

That took the wind out of my sails. Not that there was much wind left in the first place, but I wondered if I heard right. ECT? Electroconvulsive Therapy? I was dumbfounded. I staggered under the enormity of the realisation of what she had just said.

Why in the world? And how is it that nobody had told me about it? Had I been administered Electric shock? Oh God. How in the world could this happen to me?

I was silent for the rest of the day.

Dr. Madhusudan came on his rounds in the evening.

"Hello Ankita," he said, smiling in a cheerful voice. "How are you feeling?"

"Angry and cheated, doctor. Was I given ECT? And why was I not told about it? How come no one mentioned anything?" I replied sullenly.

"Oh," he said, taken aback at my direct response. He took a minute to think. Then he said that he wanted to have a talk with me and asked sister Rosaline, and two more junior doctors accompanying him to go out of the room and give us a few minutes. I noticed that the young doctor who had earlier questioned me and made detailed notes was with the group that went out of the room.

He waited till we were alone in the room. He pulled up the chair, placed it next to my bed and sat down. "Ankita," he began, "You have a severe case of bipolar disorder."

It was the first time in my life I was hearing that term.

"Let me explain how it functions. It comes in cycles. Like this," he said, as he drew a graph on the paper, which was in the writing pad that he was carrying. It looked like a wave which went up and down, much like a physics diagram that plotted some values. "Do you understand?"

I nodded.

"Right now, you are here," he said as he marked a point right at the bottom of the curve. "That is why you have attempted to kill yourself twice."

I was silent.

"It is an illness like any other illness. See, when you have a fracture, you go to an orthopaedic, right? And when you have a toothache you go to a Dentist? In the same way, when you have an illness of the mind, you come to us. People have a stigma about it. They do not understand the severity of it. People simply cannot snap out of it, they need to be treated in order to get better," he explained.

I was silent again, but he was looking into my eyes, trying to gauge if what he was saying was registering. He could see that it was beginning to sink in.

"Look, Ankita," he continued "ECT has got some very bad press but it is not at all like that. It is not how they show it in the movies. Please do not be afraid. It can be life saving and can produce dramatic results. Right now Ankita, you are at the rock bottom of the curve. In these circumstances, it is very likely that you will attempt to harm yourself again, unless we administer this. We could have put you on anti depressants but it would have taken three weeks for it to work. I really did not want to risk that. The main thing about ECT is that suicide attempts are rare after administering it. Only thing is that it has to be done twice a week. After a week we will evaluate if further treatment is needed or not."

I did not know what to say. It was the first time in months that somebody was explaining what was happening to me and assuring me that it was okay. It was the first time in months that somebody was talking to me like I mattered. It was the first time that I was being assured that I need not feel guilty for something that was out of my control.

I had agonised over not being able to 'snap out of it' and blamed myself, telling myself that it was 'all in my head' and if I wanted I could just change my thoughts and be fine again. I was being told that it was not like that at all and what I was facing now had a name, there were several people in the world much like myself who were being treated for it. It was beyond my control and I was in safe hands and would be taken care of.

The relief I was beginning to feel was like the first drops of rain on a drought filled parched earth that was beginning to crack up with the heat.

"It is going to be hard, Ankita. The feeling of worthlessness and extreme depression coupled with forces that you cannot control and that tell you to kill yourself will recur and come back to you, again and again. They are going to come in waves. You must not give in. You have to co-operate and help us to fight it. We are with you, not against you."

At that point if he had told me that holding a coconut and dancing around on one foot would make me feel better, I would have gladly believed him.

He was offering me the last vestiges of hope and I was clinging to it with the desperation of a drowning person.

20

A tiny ray of hope

To say that staying in the private room all by myself was tough would be like saying that it is hard to climb Mount Everest without capabilities of extreme levels of physical endurance. But unlike a person climbing the Everest, I had no choice in the matter at all. There was no option but to stay put. It felt surreal. The windows had strong iron grills like the cages in a zoo, probably to prevent any attempts of jumping out. There was nothing in the room with which one could hurt oneself. There was not even a table. The room just had a bed and no other piece of furniture

The emptiness of the room, in a strange way, seemed to suit the emptiness of my mind. I found the atmosphere a safe shell to which I could escape. I did not have my parents hovering over me urging me to take medication. I did not have the pressure to go back to college. I did not feel compelled to read. I did not have to do anything. My time was my own. I never expected this and was surprised to find that I had found a cocoon I could go into in and insulate myself against the harsh realities of my life. In a strange way, I was soothed.

The worst that could happen had already happened. There was nothing that could harm me anymore. The suicidal thoughts seemed like a bad nightmare now.

The doctors came on their regular rounds each morning and evening. In the morning it was the junior doctors who came. I did not talk to any of them. When they came in, I just chose to look out of the window and be silent. I did not want to talk to them or answer any questions they asked. In the evenings it was the senior doctors who came. I looked forward to these visits as Dr. Madhusudan would come each evening

Dr. Madhusudan was not only kind and understanding but intuitive too. It was almost as if he could read my mind and he knew exactly what to say to calm me down. They were mostly reassuring words of hope and inspiration. I think I owed my second shot at life, entirely to this man. He kept me alive many times over. He talked to me like I mattered. He truly cared and that made all the difference. It is indeed amazing how words and kindness have the power to heal, perhaps much more than medicines. Dr. Madhusudan had stopped all the medication which the two doctors had prescribed earlier. Instead, he put me on just a single medicine. He explained to me that it was Lithium and essential at this point that I take this tablet twice a day without fail, as it was a lifesaver for those who are bipolar. He assured me that he would take it off as soon as he felt I could cope without it. He emphasised that there was no option for me but to take it and he would gradually reduce the dosage. He told me that this was the only medicine I needed. The earlier two doctors had been treating me for severe clinical depression, but what I had was far graver. He was not only supportive but very confident that I would get better very soon, More than anything else, it was his unwavering faith in me that gave me courage.

I now had all the time in the world, to reflect on the things that I had done which had made me end up here. Dr. Madhusudan kept reassuring me that it was not 'my fault' or 'my mistake'. He said that just as people sometimes have no control over physical ailments, they have no control over mental illness. He said that it was the stigma attached to anything to do with mental health that had made him want to be a doctor.

He would always leave my room for the end, when he came on his rounds. I realised this was a pattern on the second day itself. After the preliminary talk enquiring about how I was, was over, he would dismiss the nurses and junior doctors who accompanied him. He would then ask if I minded that we have a chat. I did not mind at all. It was a welcome distraction in a room where there was nothing to do anyway. We were developing a bond which extended beyond the usual one between the doctor and the patient. I did not care. It was the last straw of hope that he was offering and I was clutching it as tightly as I could.

During one of these chats he opened up and his story shared with me which left a deep impact on me.

"Ankita, you must be thinking why this doctor takes so much interest in you, is it not?" he asked, one evening.

"Well, not really doctor. I have nothing to do here anyway. But thank you for your time, I am grateful."

"See Ankita, I come from a small village in Kerala. I think you were in Kerala earlier, isn't it?"

"Yes, I studied there for my graduation, doctor."

"So you know how society is there and how much family name

matters in a place like that. It is sometimes all that they have got," he said with a faraway look in his eyes.

I nodded. I knew exactly what he was talking about.

"I grew up in Kerala and many years back I had an elder sister. She was older to me by nearly fourteen years. When she was about 22, she committed suicide by jumping into the well which was in our backyard. On the face of it, she was well adjusted and happy. Yet there must have been things inside her mind which troubled her. Her death devastated my parents and left us in a stage of shock for the rest of our lives. We had no answers. She was a very bright student and not involved with any guy romantically as that is usually a leading cause of suicide, especially in people in that age group. Her death left a void in me which drove me to study psychiatry and I have made it my life's mission to help people who attempt suicide. Life is a gift, Ankita. We should not throw it away. You have no right to kill others. Then how can you have a right to kill yourself?" he said, his voice taking on a gentler tone.

I did not know what to say.

"I'm sorry to hear that doctor," I said finally.

"Oh no, no. Please don't be. It has only made me stronger and today I am a leading doctor. I have made my life. I want you to think about yours. Nothing is lost just because you dropped out of MBA. It is not the be-all and end-all of life. You can still do other things in life, Ankita" he said.

That was the first time such an option had struck me. Till now, my parents had pinned their hopes on my going back to complete my course. I knew that I did not want to go back. The question of alternatives had not even occurred to me since I had been so disturbed. Now Dr. Madhusudan had given me something to think about. It was a seed that he had sown and it had taken firm root. For the first time in many months, I thought about the future and what other things I could do if I did not complete my MBA. It was the first time in months that a faint fluttering of hope had begun stirring in me. It was a small ray of sunlight which was peeping in enticingly through a slight crack in the door which had caught me in its tight grip. I was ready to move towards it.

When he came the next day I decided to open up and speak and give voice to my deepest fears.

"Doctor, I have been thinking about what you said," I began.

He nodded encouragingly.

"The thing is I seem to have lost my ability to read and comprehend. I do want to study. In fact I so much want to study. But nothing I read is able to stay in my mind. Nothing makes sense anymore doctor. It frightens me when I try to open a book and read. Here, I feel safe. I am content. I am very afraid about what will happen when I get discharged," I said.

"Ankita, you will not be sent to your house directly. You have just taken the first step now. You have just survived one of the most terrifying mental ordeals a human being can face. You are still recouping. At the end of the week, you will be shifted into the Occupational Therapy wing. We have a huge wing which is at the other end of the campus. It is best you be there for at least a month. We will put you on a program that will truly help you and trust me, all this will just seem like a bad dream very soon," He said reassuringly.

"Will you be coming on the rounds there, doctor?" I asked him. That was the only concern which I had at that point of time. Doctor Madhusudan was my lifeline and I did not want to stop seeing him.

"Actually different doctors are in charge there. I look after this ward,"

My heart sank hearing those words. I could not imagine getting through the day without speaking to him. I think he sensed it too.

"But I will surely be visiting you very regularly after my rounds here," he said.

My face lit up with a smile. It was the first time in months that I had smiled.

By the end of that week, they shifted me to the other side of the campus which had the Occupational therapy wing, popularly called the O.T wing.

O.T wing seemed like a different world altogether. It did not have the feel of a hospital in the least bit. In fact one could not even see the Hospital building from this wing as the campus was spread over more than 80 acres of land and the O.T wing was far removed from the main hospital. It was a huge building with colonial architecture, much like a holiday home or a resort. It was spread out on a single floor. It had beautiful gardens and well manicured lawns in the front. There were marigolds, azaleas, lilies and many other colourful flowers blooming in the flower beds and patches. It had a cheery feel, completely different from the hospital and I was very surprised when I first saw it. I was shown to my room, which had two single beds, a desk, a chair and even a mirror in the bathroom. There was stationery on the table, two pens and pencils. There was a pretty tiny porcelain flower vase on the table with two yellow flowers whose names I did not know in it. They brightened up the place and added a nice warm touch. There was also a chart on the table which had a printed 'routine schedule' which had been planned for me. It read as follows:

Name: Ankita Sharma

Doctor: Madhusudan Jairam

Routine:

6.30 A.M.	:	Wake up time, brushing teeth, personal grooming
7.30 A.M.	:	Morning walk
8.30 A.M.	:	Breakfast
10:00-11:00 A.M.	:	Doctors rounds. You are requested to be in your room at this time.
11.00- 12.30 P.M.	:	Recreational Hall
12.30-2.30 P.M.	:	Lunch time
2.30-4.30 P.M.	:	Leisure. You can utilise this time to do whatever you want to
4.30-6.30 P.M	:	Gardening or outdoor Sports
6.30-7.30 P.M.	:	Psychotherapy
7.30-8.30 P.M.	:	Reading, recreation, rest, yoga
8.30-9.45 P.M.	:	Dinner
10.30 P.M.	:	Bed time

I was surprised to see such a well-planned routine. After weeks of having nothing to do, this was a kind of jolt to me, but it did not disturb me or make me feel agitated. In fact, I was happy to have something to do finally. Something, where I did not have to think about how to fill my empty hours and the emptiness in my life.

I was worried only about one thing. I did not want my parents to visit me. I did not feel like seeing them yet. I felt that the negativity and all the unstated and dormant hopes about completing my MBA would come back with them, if they came to see me. When the attendant showed me to my room, my worry was laid to rest as he confirmed this, "Madam, have you requested no visitors to be allowed?" he asked.

I nodded.

Then I had to sign a form which declared that I did not want any visitors at this point in time. I signed it willingly and hoped that my parents would not be hurt and would understand.

I was thrown into the 'routine' planned for me straight away. It was about 10.30 A.M. when I had been shown into my room. I barely had time to settle down and absorb my new surroundings, when the attendant came knocking on all the doors.

"Oooooo teeeee...Oooooo teeeee. Recreation room, recreation room," he called out in a sing song voice as he knocked on all doors, including mine.

The other occupants of the rooms had come out too. There was a very stylishly dressed slim woman, who wore a short skirt, stilettos and was strikingly good looking. Her nails were perfectly manicured and her complexion was almost translucent. She followed the attendant without so much as a glance at the others. There was a young man who was bone thin and sported a shaggy beard and a Kurta. There was a middle aged man, slightly overweight who had begun balding. There was an elderly lady who looked defeated. There were two young men in the group who were well dressed and looked perfectly normal. They were talking to each other. The bone thin young man was talking to the elderly lady. It seemed they knew each other well. All of us followed the attendant to the recreation room.

The recreation room had a wide range of activities to choose from. There was scrabble, chess and carrom. There was a table tennis table on one side. There were comfortable sofas. There was a television and a video player too. All the latest magazines were laid out neatly. On one side of the room, there were sheets of papers and crayons and art material. I was totally taken aback to see all this. Looking at it, nobody would have said that this was a place for a bunch of mental health patients all on the road to recovery. We all seemed perfectly fine and fit.

We were a motley group who had been thrown together by circumstances. The others seemed to have their preferred activities. The elderly lady took out a ball of dark brown wool and sat knitting silently. I wondered what she was making and who it was for.

The gorgeous looking woman headed towards the magazines and began reading. All the others too busied themselves in various games and activities.

I stood there uncertainly, wondering what to do. Finally I was drawn towards the table which had the art material.

I looked at the papers, the crayons and paints, laid out along with the brushes. I touched them hesitatingly, still unsure. It seemed like months since I had last used colours. At one time they had been so important in my life. Now I began to feel faint but slightly familiar urges. I remembered the joy I had felt when I had first painted the water fall. I remembered the feeling of being alive that I had, when I had painted. I remembered the happy emotions I had experienced. More than anything, I remembered that I had once been joyous, hopeful, content and happy. I wanted all of it back. I wanted this deadness to end.

And suddenly I wanted to paint once more.

21

Faith is a powerful thing

It felt strange to be holding paintbrush once again. I did not know what to paint. I looked outside the window and saw rows of flowers nodding their heads happily in the sunshine. Finally that was what I painted. It was a quick impression of those flowers. A splatter of red and yellow. I added green too. Then I painted the sky light blue. I worked fast and furiously. I slapped on paint like I had never seen before. I was so absorbed in my picture and that I did not realise it was lunch time. When I turned around I saw the two young men I had seen earlier, standing behind me and looking at my picture.

"It's good," said the taller of the two.

The other one nodded appreciatively.

"Thank you," I managed to say. I was not sure that I wanted an audience for my work. I had just begun coming out of my cocoon and did not want to speak to anyone. I hoped they would leave me alone. But they took my acknowledgement as a signal to talk.

"Hi. I am Sagar," said the taller one.

"And I am Anuj," said the other.

"Hi," I managed to say, avoiding eye contact. I hoped they would get the hint and leave me alone. I pretended to add finishing touches to the picture. I could still see them from the corner of my eye. They weren't budging.

"And you are...?" said Sagar.

"Ankita," I answered, still bent over my picture.

"It is lunch time now. We have to go to the dining hall," said Anuj.

I went along with them to the dining hall.

I helped myself to some rice, some curry and some vegetables. It was the first time in months that I actually noticed what I was eating. Till now, food was consumed simply because I had to stay alive. But now I actually noticed that the vegetables indeed looked delicious. The curry was a fiery red, but it was not as hot as it looked. It was tangy and tasty. The rice was cooked just right. It was light and fluffy. It felt like heaven in my mouth. Or perhaps it seemed that way to me. It was like a dead person coming to life after a very long while and then tasting food. I took a morsel and then stared at the food on my plate for a few seconds before I joined Anuj and Sagar, my new friends, at their table as they motioned me to join them.

Then we conversed about movies and about books. Both Sagar and Anuj were avid readers and had watched almost all the movies that I had, much like everybody else in our age group. I discovered that I could converse easily. Nobody asked any questions about why I was there and what my past was. Perhaps that was an unsaid understanding that existed amongst everybody there. I felt happy about that. It gave me a feeling of security. I would have hated it, had they probed and I would then have withdrawn into my shell. But they were easy going and friendly and it was hard not to be drawn into their talk and laughter.

Later in my room, I wondered why they were in O.T. They seemed perfectly sane and normal to me. It did not seem they had any mental health issues or any problem. They were just two regular guys. Suddenly it occurred to me that I would have appeared the same to anyone who looked at me.

The realisation was like an epiphany. It gave me a jolt. I *was* in fact 'normal'! If I pretended to be 'normal' and behaved just like everybody else, if I masked my emotions and I smiled a lot, even if I felt disconsolate, *nobody would be able to tell.* I made up my mind right then, that if that was all it took to be termed 'normal', that was how it would be from now on. No matter what I felt, I would never show it. I would pretend everything was fine. I no longer felt as suicidal as I had done earlier. Maybe it was the lithium or maybe it was the O.T routine. But I knew I was feeling definitely better than before.

The road from the coldness of the isolated prison that I had been trapped in, to this 'safe zone' which I was in now, had been a very rocky one. It had not been easy at all. It had nearly taken my life. But the fact was that I had made it and I was here now.

I discovered from Anuj and Sagar that during the 4.30-6.30 evening slot, one could either opt for volleyball, basketball or badminton in sports. If one did not want to play, one could do gardening. You had a choice of planting something in your own patch, which you would be allotted if you opted for gardening. But if you did not want to do it on your own, you could tend to the common plants in the garden. The garden was indeed beautiful.

While I enjoyed admiring and painting the flowers, I knew instantly that it was sports I would opt for. Sagar did not play but preferred gardening. Anuj played basketball and I decided to play with him.

Playing with Anuj that evening, every nerve in my body pulsated with life. Anuj won easily. I was panting and struggling to keep up with him. But, oh the joy! I felt so alive as sweat trickled down my forehead as I ran, playing my best. It had been very long since I had any kind of physical exercise and my muscles stretched and groaned as they were compelled back into action. I revelled in it, savoured it and glowed in the effort of the game. Later, we sat on the hard cement floor of the court, utterly worn out but thoroughly satisfied. I wiped the sweat off my face and drank cool water from a plastic bottle that Sagar brought to us, after his gardening. It felt like nectar.

"You two have 15 minutes to get out of those sweat drenched clothes and get ready," said Sagar.

"The game was so good I had almost forgotten we have PT," replied Anuj.

I figured out that it stood for psychotherapy when Sagar asked if I knew which doctor was assigned to me.

"I guess it must be Dr. Madhusudan," I said. At least I hoped so.

"Usually it is only the junior doctors who come for psycho therapy. Dr. Madhusudan is very senior. Mine is Anjana Thomas. She is good," said Anuj.

"Oh yeah! Don't we all know it!" said Sagar and I smiled.

It occurred to me that we were discussing psychotherapy and doctors like we used to discuss subjects and professors in college.

The psychotherapy sessions involved talking to whichever doctor was assigned to you. I hoped like mad that I would see Dr. Madhusudan. He had promised me that he would come and see me. I hoped he was not too busy and would remember. But my hopes were short-lived as I discovered that it was a junior doctor called Namita Deshmukh who was assigned to me.

"Hello Ankita. Do come in and sit down. I am Dr. Namita," she said pleasantly and I noticed that the smile reached her eyes. She wore a saree and had a melodious voice. It looked like she meant her welcome but I was not completely at ease.

Then I noticed my file on her table.

"Ankita, I want to assure you that you are doing very well and we are all here to support you," she said.

I nodded. I hated the fact that she had seen my life. I did not like that every bit of my past was written in those papers and she knew everything about it. I did not mind discussing it with Dr. Madhusudan, but I felt Dr. Namita had no right to know any of the past events that had changed my life so. It was as though she read my mind.

"Dr. Madhusudan has a special interest in your case and he will be here soon. He assigned me to you, and told me to fill in till he comes. We need not talk about anything if you don't want. We can just talk about movies or anything else that interests you."

I was not sure how to react to her words. Finally I told her that I would wait for Dr. Madhusudan .We sat in silence and I think she was more uncomfortable than I was, because she did not know what to do.

Dr. Madhusudan arrived after about ten minutes. I was overjoyed to see him.

"Thank you Namita," he said as he dismissed her and as she left I found myself relaxing instantly.

Dr. Madhusudan could see that too.

"Ankita, all the doctors are trained to help. Dr. Namita is very sweet and efficient. I had personally assigned her to your case. She has made an in depth study of your file," he said.

"But doctor, that is precisely what is making me uncomfortable!" I exclaimed.

"Everything in the file is confidential, Ankita and I must assure you that only the doctors assigned to the case will have access to the personal information files," he said.

That reassured me somewhat.

Then Dr. Madhusudan said that I was very talented and had a great gift for writing. He said I ought to nurture it. He also said my paintings were good and I should take it up further.

I was puzzled. How had Dr. Madhusudan known about my writing? There was only one way to know and I asked him.

"Ankita, the forty two page letter that you wrote to your friend was what gave us a clue about it. The letter had some brilliant lines and some superb prose. I am sorry we had to go through it all. We also studied your pictures. The ones you painted. " Dr. Madhusudan said.

I was baffled. How did the letter that I had written to Suvi reach them? How did they get my paintings? Oh my God! I had poured out my heart in that letter. It was not meant for anybody else's eyes other than Suvi's. How could she betray me like this? I was hurt, upset, annoyed yet a strange kind of relief also flooded through me, because now there was nothing more that I could hide from Dr.

Madhusudan anymore. It felt liberating in a very strange manner. All my defences were laid bare. I was vulnerable and totally exposed, yet I felt completely safe.

"Ankita, your father was very worried about your behaviour while you were in Bombay. The suicide attempts disturbed him no end as it would disturb any parent. Your father is a pro-active person and he contacted your friend Suvi. He explained the whole situation to her. He had to convince her a lot about the gravity of the situation. Finally she mailed him a photocopy of the letter you wrote which is what we have in the file here. It was the letter which first pointed me in the direction of bipolar disorder. Yours is not a typical text book case, Ankita. This was why the earlier doctors who treated you were thrown off the track."

I sat silently absorbing all that he had said. I imagined the letter being analysed and dissected. I pictured the doctors discussing the letter and then using medical terms to find patterns to a psychological disorder. I felt sick picturing it. I felt humiliated. I winced inwardly. Yet this dissection was what gave them an indication of what I was going through. This was what guided them in the right direction and they could control it and help me get out of its grip. I was confused now and the thoughts were going round in my head.

Dr. Madhusudan again sensed what I must have been thinking. Perhaps he had that rare understanding and sensitivity or perhaps he had that rapport with me. He seemed to know exactly what I was thinking and how I felt.

"Ankita, do you know something? Creativity is closely associated with bipolar disorder. This condition is unique. Many famous historical figures and artists have had this. Yet they have led a full life and contributed so much to the society and world at large. See, you have a gift. People with bipolar disorder are very very sensitive. Much more than ordinary people. They are able to experience emotions in a very deep and intense way. It gives them a very different perspective of the world. It is not that they lose touch with reality. But the feelings of extreme intensity are manifested in creating things. They pour their emotions into either writing or art or whatever field they have chosen. Have you heard of Vincent Van Gogh, Ankita?" he asked. His voice was full of tenderness and concern.

Of course I had heard of Vincent Van Gogh. I had admired his work and I was astounded by its simplicity and depth when I had first come across it. I had in fact, borrowed one of the art books from my school library while at school and had attempted to copy his paintings.

"Oh yes doctor, he is one of my favourite artists!" I exclaimed in joy, smiling at the memory.

"Well, he too had bipolar disorder," said Dr. Madhusudan.

"Oh!" I said, the revelation taking me by complete surprise. I had not known anything about Van Gogh's personal life. The book that I had borrowed was mostly a collection of his paintings and had not mentioned anything about his personal life.

Dr. Madhusudan's words had found their mark and now I was beginning to feel very important and special.

"In a fit of extreme emotion, Van Gogh had cut off his ear" said Dr. Madhusudan.

That piece of information which was also new to me brought me back to the painful reality of the illness in a jiffy.

I could now understand fully why he would have done that. He must have been helpless, caught in a vortex, like I had been, just a fortnight ago, when I had no control over my emotions. I could feel his helplessness and sense his pain.

"Ankita, this is going to come to you in cycles. There will be highs and there will be lows. You have just experienced the highs when you were at your creative best and unstoppable. Then you experienced the lows which almost took your life. What we are doing here is helping you regulate it, so that you can manage it yourself. This is just the first brush you have had with it. There may be future episodes and you have to be prepared. We are here for you, to help you," said Dr. Madhusudan.

The enormity of whatever he had said was sinking in slowly and spreading in my mind like darkness after sunset. Till then it had not occurred to me that I might have to battle it once more. I had presumed that the worse was over and it was behind me.

Yet I had implicit faith in Dr. Madhusudan's words. I felt if he said I could manage it, I would. I believed him with all my heart. Sometimes all one needs is a strong anchor, a person you can trust blindly. Someone who will lead you on, be there for you and never let you down. To me Dr. Madhusudan was that person. His presence calmed me. His words reassured me. I trusted him completely.

"You are a very brave girl, Ankita," he said as he patted my hand.

Faith is a strange and a powerful thing and it can work miracles.

It was something I would soon discover.

22

One step at a time

The next morning when the doctors came on their rounds Dr. Namita came along. She carried in her hand a large plastic bag. When the doctors finished their routine questions and were leaving, Dr. Namita stayed back.

"This is for you Ankita. Dr. Madhusudan told me to give it to you," She said as she handed over the packet to me. He has also asked me to work with you from 2.30 to 4.30 P.M. everyday. I'll see you here in the afternoon at 2.30 sharp," she said as she left.

As soon as she left, I opened the packet. It contained a set of children's books. They looked old but were in perfect condition. Most were Russian books translated into English with fascinating illustrations. The titles were very interesting and I had never seen books like them before.

There was a book titled "Within and without wears his coat wrong side out."

Then there was another which said "Baba Yaga and other stories".

There was a third book by Alexander Raskin which said "When daddy was a little boy".

Then there was a book for teenagers called "Masha Nikiforova's days." There were also books of Brer Rabbit and Winnie the Pooh.

I was surprised to find that Dr. Madhusudan had sent me such an assorted and rare collection. I did not know what to make of it till I saw his note.

"One step at a time, Ankita. We're getting there!" He had scrawled on a tiny bit of paper in his spidery handwriting which spread across it.

I could not resist opening the books. The first thing that I saw when I opened the first book were the words in a child's writing "*This book belongs to Madhusudan Jairam and Vibha Jairam.*" Beneath it was an address in Kerala. It was evident that the books belonged to Dr. Madhusudan's childhood. I also guessed that Vibha must have been his sister as they shared the same surname and the address. It made me feel sad as I could picture that little girl whose hands must have held this book many years back. Who would have thought that she would take her own life? I felt emotional as I turned the page.

What I saw took my breath away. The Illustrations were simply fantastic and nothing like I had ever seen before! I gazed in amazement and wonder at the beautiful and exotic pictures. The pictures were full of details. The colours were vibrant. Some of the pictures were black and white and had an eerie, deathlike quality about them, as they were full of hatchings and cross hatchings. I was so absorbed in looking at the illustrations that I did not realise how time had passed. The attendant was calling out that it was time for recreation room. It was with great reluctance that I put the books away.

I did not have much time to think about them as we had to go to the recreation room. I walked along with Anuj and Sagar. I painted another picture. This time I painted the sofa in the room. I also painted the elderly lady who was knitting. I did not paint the features on her face but it was obvious that I had painted her from the clothes she was wearing and the pose she had adopted. Anuj and Sagar admired it once more dutifully.

"You are good at this! You paint well!" said Sagar.

These guys were so good for my ego! I felt happy to be appreciated.

Before I realised it, lunch hour had passed and it was time to go back to the room.

Dr. Namita was already there when I came back from lunch.

"Hi Ankita," she smiled brightly.

"Hello doctor," I replied. I was feeling a bit friendlier towards her, after my talk with Dr. Madhusudan.

"Do call me Namita. Doctor sounds so formal," she smiled. That statement of hers won me over and I smiled.

"Ankita, I am here to help you with the reading and the writing." She said a matter of factly. There were no judgements passed here and there was not a trace of pity or condescension in her voice. I liked that. I wasn't sure what she had in mind but I had a vague notion why Dr. Madhusudan had sent me the books.

"Are you able to read those books?" asked Namita.

"I have only looked at the pictures so far. I have not tried reading the books."

"Let's do it. Choose any one."

I looked at the books. At one time, my desk had been filled with Kotler and other management books. Now it was children's books.

It is hard to describe how I felt. At one time reading and words had been the core of my existence. I had prided myself on my memory and intellect. Now I seemed to be back to square one. It was almost as though I was reduced to the level of a six year old who had just learnt to read. There was no way out from here. Dr. Madhusudan believed in me. His reassurances of my getting back to my old self soothed me. I could not let him down. I made up my mind. If reading children's books was what it took, to get back my reading and comprehension abilities, I would do that. I had to make a beginning somewhere.

"Ok," I said and I picked up 'Masha Nikiforova's days'.

"Let me get another chair for this room, and then we can use the table," said Dr. Namita as she called out to the attendant to fetch a chair. He was back with a wooden chair in no time.

Dr. Namita pulled the table towards her, away from the wall and positioned her chair on one side. She motioned me to sit down. It was a little like a tutor working with a single student.

I opened the book and read the first lines

"*I'm starting my diary today. Actually I decided to start one long ago, last month, or even before that. I found twenty kopecks today. The coin was lying on the sidewalk, and there was nobody near it.*"

But by the time I reached the end of the second sentence, I could hardly remember what the first sentence was. I was reading but I had no idea what it meant. I went back and read the first sentence. Then the second one again. But once again the words vanished from my mind and I was left gasping for a meaning, for a nuance, for the paragraph to make sense. Tears of frustration welled up in my eyes.

Why wasn't I able to read and retain a simple sentence? Is this how the rest of my life is going to be? Why am I not able to follow a children's book?

I controlled my tears and told Dr. Namita "I cannot do this. I am not able to go on."

"Ankita, you will just have to try harder. Come on now, do it once more," she said gently but firmly.

I tried again. And yet again. It was the same result as before. My attention span and concentration were really affected. I was terrified. Had my brain been damaged? Why was this happening?

I had been reading the same two sentences over and over again, trying to make sense of it, failing miserably.

Dr. Namita could see my frustration and could sense my pain.

"Okay Ankita, let us do one thing. I will dictate and you write down what I am saying, ok?" she said.

"Yes," I barely managed to say.

Dr. Namita chose the Brer rabbit book. She began dictating just two words at a time. I had no trouble writing them down. She then said the next two words. Again I had no trouble following it. When I finished writing the sentence, I was able to retain what it meant. We worked in silence like this for about forty five minutes. I had written out the entire book.

Finally Dr. Namita said that it was enough for the day.

"Ankita, you have been under tremendous stress in the past months. Don't worry. You are making good progress. I will come back tomorrow," she said as she left.

After she left, I stared at the words I had written. Then I broke down. My body shook with nerve wracking sobs. The cry sounded to my own ears like a primeval cry for help. It was a cry of pure pain and helplessness. I felt anguished that I had been reduced to this state of having to *write out* a children's book, before my brain could retain the information. I had prided myself on my intellect. I had felt elated when I had topped the IT test in my MBA course and when I had first cleared the management entrance tests. I compared what I had once been to what I had been reduced to and the tears continued flowing. Gradually the sobs eased. I got up and washed my face when I heard the attendant knocking on the door calling out for outdoor time.

Anuj and Sagar took one look at me and I knew they had seen my blood shot eyes.

I think, spending time in a mental health Institution makes you a hundredfold more sensitive towards others than you were earlier. You learn to value emotions. You learn to look out for others. You learn to truly care. Most importantly you learn to pay heed to what others *do not* tell you.

I was taken aback when Anuj put his hands around my shoulder and said gently in a soft voice "Hey, don't be too harsh on yourself. It is okay."

I was afraid that his kindness would unleash a fresh flood of tears but I managed to hold them back.

"You see that guy there?" asked Sagar, pointing to the tall lanky bearded man.

I nodded.

"He was a senate member in the Academic council at Stanford University. Can you believe it? He has a wife and a young child. They visit him on weekends. He had a nervous breakdown and that is why he is here now, recovering," he said.

"And you know that lady? The one who is always stylishly dressed?" asked Anuj.

I nodded again.

"She has an eating disorder. She has two children too. Her husband and her children are waiting for her to get better. You should see the joy on her children's faces when they visit her. That is the only time I have seen her smile," said Anuj.

"How do both of you know all these details? " I asked.

"We have been around a lot longer here than you," said Anuj.

I felt immensely grateful to them for the things they said. But more than that I loved the fact that they had not magnified either their ordeal or mine. They had not talked about themselves. Nor had they prodded me or even made me feel that I had to explain myself. They made me feel 'okay'. I cherished that. It was a feeling that I had not had for a very long time. I loved them for it.

After that, the routine which had been set for me continued. Life went on like a train on tracks, governed by the Railway timetable. Anuj and I played basketball and Sagar did his gardening, as usual, till it was time for psychotherapy. Dr. Madhusudan was there this time. We talked about my effort in reading for the day. Dr. Madhusudan praised me and said it was a baby step in the right direction. He encouraged me to try hard and not feel frustrated. He said my system had taken a huge shock and emphasised that I would get back all the abilities that I had—it was just that I had to work towards it. It did not seem that way to me, but I desperately wanted to believe him. He was offering me a lever called hope and I grabbed it.

Six whole weeks passed in this manner. I was getting better each day. By the end of the sixth week, I discovered that I no longer needed to write out the passages from the books to remember the previous sentences. I was overjoyed! If someone had told me I had won the National lottery I don't think I would have been as thrilled. This was truly the best thing that had happened to me in a very long time.

At one single sitting, I read *Masha Nikiforova's days* from the beginning to the end. I just could not stop! The thrill of being able to finish a book and comprehend it perfectly matched no joy that I had known before. I simply could not believe it! I felt like dancing and shouting out to the world and telling everyone who passed by "Look I am able to read! Look I am able to remember!"

But of course, I controlled my emotions and pretended it was just another day. Nobody would have been able to understand the depth of my joy and the extent of my happiness unless they had themselves gone through what I just had. I hugged my little secret to myself and I hoarded the books as a miser hoards his treasure. I couldn't wait to get time to myself, so that could finish all the books. I was like a thirsty traveller in a desert who had finally got around the mirages and managed to reach the oasis.

That evening I broke the news to Dr. Madhusudan. He was as delighted as I was.

"That is indeed wonderful Ankita! Well done!" he said. Then he asked me if I was ready to meet my parents. He said that my parents had been often checking on me by getting in touch with him. But I still was not ready as yet. I told him to defer it by a few more days. I also asked Dr. Madhusudan if he could get me more books and this time I did not want children's books.

"Yes, I have a collection in my office. I will send them through Dr. Namita" he promised.

The regular physical exercise and the routine set had been silently working wonders on my weight. When I looked into the mirror one morning I was surprised to see a glowing complexion and a peaceful expression. I smiled at myself as I brushed my hair. Suddenly I felt wonderful and thankful to be alive.

That evening Anuj and Sagar had a gift for me. I was pleasantly surprised and touched.

"What is the occasion?" I asked them trying to guess what was inside the nicely wrapped packet.

"You don't need an occasion to make others feel good, Ankita. Life is a celebration!" said Anuj.

"Now you sound like a new age guru. All you need is some saffron robes," I teased.

But I was secretly pleased to see the effort they had made. Their gift was two cassettes which were volume one and two of "The world's greatest love songs". There were a few of the latest numbers as well as all the classics. The songs were all feel-good songs.

"Nice! Thank you." I said.

"And you can listen to them tonight—ta-da" said Anuj as he produced a tape recorder from behind his back. "This is not a gift! I am just lending it to you," he clarified quickly and I smiled.

That night I drifted off to sleep with Elvis Presley singing in his melancholic voice "Are you lonesome tonight?"

Are you lonesome tonight,
Do you miss me tonight?
Are you sorry we drifted apart?

His voice filled the room and my mind raced back to those memories when Vaibhav had played the song "Nothing's gonna stop us now" on my birthday.

I couldn't help thinking what a long way I had come and how much I had grown up since then. It seemed like a lifetime to me.

Life was indeed unpredictable and it was true that it could take a sudden unexpected turn. I contemplated in silence and kept one hand on my precious books that I had placed next to my pillow, as I fell asleep that night.

23

I am the master of my fate

Finally, it was time to leave. I felt a slight sense of trepidation as well as happiness. I was happy that my ordeal was over and I was now 'free'. But I felt bad about leaving behind the world that had been my home for the past many weeks.

Dr. Madhusudan had prepared me well. He said I had made remarkable progress and it was because of my strong will power and determination alone that I had bounced back so quickly. I was still on Lithium which I had to take just once a day for the next two months. After that, he had tapered the course to be taken and it would have to be taken every alternate day, for the next two weeks. Then it would be every third day. Finally it would be twice a week, then once a week and then I could stop taking it altogether. Dr. Madhusudan emphasised that it was extremely important that I did not discontinue the medicine. He warned me that I would feel fine and I would be tempted to stop taking the medication. He spoke to me about a lot of people who seemed to be getting better but had worsened suddenly simply because they had either discontinued the medicine or given up too quickly.

"And Ankita, you have a real talent for writing as well as painting. Do something about it. Do not waste it. Not everybody is gifted. You are and you are indeed lucky," he said.

"Ha ha. May be I will write a book someday, Doctor. If I do, I would surely write about you," I joked as I brushed his compliment aside. I was embarrassed and I did not know how to handle it.

He looked straight into my eyes. "I would be very proud of you, if you do it, Ankita," he said.

I did not know what to say and so I mumbled an incoherent reply and muttered a thank you.

Then I took out the card that I had made for him the previous day at the recreation room.

I had painted a burning flame on the face of the card, which was surrounded by a bluish green light. Inside I had written

To Dr. Madhusudan who went beyond the call of duty.

I owe you a lot. You have taught me the value of life, and you have taught me that love and time are the greatest gifts one can receive. I have put a lot of time and a lot more of my love into these paintings which I have made. There was a time when I could not paint and could not write. Now I can and I hold them dearer than life itself. I guess you, of all people, would know completely, what I mean when I say this. To me, this is the greatest gift I can ever give somebody. I hope you like them.

With love and warmest regards

Ankita

I had chosen three of my best pictures, out of all the ones that I had been painting and I had wrapped them carefully with old newspaper.

Dr. Madhusudan opened the card right there. He read the card first and then looked at the paintings. He spread them on his desk and gazed at them.

He was silent for a long time. I could see he was moved.

Then he swallowed once and he said "Ankita, I shall truly cherish them. They are beautiful. Thank you. These will be framed and displayed on the walls in my office. And I do wish you the very best in life. Mark my words, you will do well."

I had made a card for Dr. Namita too. It was a simple thank you card with the picture of a flower on it.

I had not made cards for Anuj or Sagar but decided to gift them my paintings. For Sagar, I had chosen two pictures which showed his beloved garden he so loved working in. For Anuj, I chose one which showed a view of the basketball court and another which showed the building which had been home to all of us, for the past few weeks.

They were delighted with my gift.

"Thank you Ankita," said Sagar and he hugged me tight. He almost crushed me and I hugged him back. I could feel his love and his genuine friendship in that hug.

"And where is my hug? Only he gets to hug you, is it?" asked Anuj in mock anger.

I laughed as I hugged him and planted a kiss on his cheek. He was taken by surprise for a few seconds and then he kissed me right back on both my cheeks. He then jumped up in the air and pumped his fist and said "whoo hoooo" as I laughed in delight at his antics.

"This is not fair, by the way," said Sagar.

"What? Kissing him?" I asked genuinely surprised.

"No, you silly! You come in here, after us and now you leave before us. Now what are we supposed to do without you?" said Sagar.

"I am sure you will leave soon too. Or would you rather I stay here?" I half joked. A part of me did want to stay on.

"Don't even joke about it," said Anuj.

"You know Ankita, when people joke about how they think they should be admitted in mental hospital or how they think they should be on Valium, it takes a great deal of effort for me to smile," said Sagar.

I knew exactly what he was talking about. I hoped Anuj and Sagar would get to leave soon, as well. It wasn't a topic we wanted to talk about, so we changed it and continued talking about movies and other things, as usual.

That evening we talked for a very long time. It was as though we wanted these few precious hours that we had left together, to last for a lifetime.

Finally when it was time to go I hugged them again and said my goodbyes.

It was raining the next day when my parents came to pick me up.

They were waiting in the recreation room. Dr. Madhusudan was there too.

My parents suddenly looked a lot older than I remembered them. It was a very emotional moment. We weren't used to expressing our love in our family and instead of hugging them I stood there stupidly staring at my feet.

Dr. Madhusudan summed up the entire thing he had told me about the importance of continuing Lithium. He then told my dad to be in touch on the phone. My parents were genuinely grateful to this man as much as I was. My dad promised to be in touch.

We flew back to Bombay the same day.

My parents were now treating me with extra care and concern, like I was fragile. While I enjoyed their extra care and attention, the fact was I was a lot tougher now, than I had ever been earlier.

My earlier ambition had been to complete MBA and to prove myself in the corporate world. Suddenly, after what I had been through, it all seemed meaningless to me. I couldn't stand the thought of going back to MBA. I had grown up in so many ways since the time I first joined the course. I thought about my classmates and professors. I thought about the text books and case studies. The more I thought about it, the more meaningless they all seemed to me. It was as though I had been looking at life through a keyhole earlier and seeing only the MBA bit. But now the whole door had been thrown open. My perspective had changed a lot. It was a paradigm shift in my approach to life itself.

My dad tried his best to convince me to go back. He reminded me that he had already paid the fees for the academic year. I felt sorry about it but I emphasised that I would not go back. I had decided to drop out of the course. An MBA from a premier institute was not everything in life. Life was far bigger. I had truly learnt the value of life in these past few weeks.

How could I make my parents understand that? How would they know I had changed and had grown? How would they ever relate to whatever I had gone through? How could I tell them the sheer agony in writing out children's' books page by page to comprehend them? How could I tell them what a large mountain I had scaled? How could I tell them that I now valued my paintings and my ability to read and my words more than I valued anything else?

I explained to my dad that I had thought about it and I had now made up my mind. I would take two months off and then I would enrol in a Creative writing course. It was something that had always interested me. I would love to study further but now on I would do only those things that made me happy and filled me with joy.

My parents could see how I had changed and they could now see the strength in me. I was so sure now of what I wanted in life. Life was too precious to *not* do the things one wanted to. I made enquiries at Bombay University and enrolled for the course which was to begin in two months. It was a one year post graduate diploma and also involved a practical stint with a media house. One could either write articles for a newspaper or a magazine depending on what one was interested in. It sounded exciting to me as it meant my words would reach thousands of readers. By the end of two months, my medication would have completely stopped too. I looked forward to the course and couldn't wait for it to begin.

My parents told me that Vaibhav had called many times while I was in the hospital. They had not told him that I was in the hospital. They had said that I needed a break and was in Kerala, visiting relatives. He had asked for a number where he could reach me and my mother had said that I was in a village where there were no phones. I loved her for wanting to protect me. I was now seeing my parents in a new light too. I felt very bad and regretful for the pain I had inflicted on them. I could now see how hard it must have been for them, to watch me go through it all. But the thing is we had all emerged stronger because of it.

My parents were now a lot more open towards my friends. Perhaps they had realised how important a part my friends had played in my life. But it was not something we talked about. It was unspoken but understood.

Now there was only one thing left to do. I had to write to Vaibhav and explain my long silence.

I felt powerful and triumphant as I took out a paper and a pen and paused for a few moments, soaking in the exhilaration of being able to write and express myself. Writing was something I had taken for granted earlier. I had not even thought about it, but now I valued each word like a precious gem.

I chose beautiful handmade paper and began writing.

Dearest Vaibhav,

It has been such a long time since I wrote and I am sure you have given up all hopes of hearing from me. My mother tells me you called many times. Thank you for the care and concern. A lot has happened in these past months. I have no idea where to begin.

My last letter to you probably described my course and how well I was doing. But, the latest from my end is that I have decided to drop out of my MBA. Yes—I can picture you being shocked and asking me why.

It is a very long story, Vaibhav. I'd probably have to talk to you for hours to explain why.

Sometimes, we do not appreciate fully what we have unless we lose it. With me too, it has been the same. I thought I was the greatest when I managed to get into the MBA course. I prided myself on my smartness and my intellectual ability. Perhaps in my arrogance, I had considered myself superior to many others who had not made it—who knows! I had presumed that having a corporate career is the ultimate thing is life. To go up the ladder, reach a high position, be financially independent and roll in the big bucks that a campus placement will bring you.

But Vaibhav, I am so much wiser now. I am no longer the same starry eyed Ankita who attended the fresher's induction programme at my course. I have changed in many ways and at levels deeper than I myself can comprehend.

My last few weeks have been spent in the occupational therapy wing of NMHI. I survived two suicide attempts. I have been to hell and back and what is more, I am proud to say I have lived to tell the tale.

In case you don't know NMHI is the best care for mental health in India. People come from all over the world over to get treated here. Strangely Vaibhav, the last few weeks at OT wing have been the happiest in my life. For the first time in my life I felt I was doing something worthwhile with my time.

I do not think anyone will fully comprehend what exactly happened to me unless they have themselves gone through what I have. Here I was, a 'smart, promising young lady' who suddenly had 'mental health issues' and had to drop out. I know this is how the world would probably see it. The thing is I do not care anymore.

There is only a fine line between sanity and insanity. Who is to decide that someone is insane and others are 'normal'? If somebody does not conform to set norms of behaviour, the society terms them as eccentric, odd, mad and crazy. Is it really fair? There is a stigma attached to anything to do with mental health. There is so much fear and so many misapprehensions. I know, because I have seen it myself.

Vaibhav, because of my stay at the OT wing, I can see beauty in life. Each day, I feel, is a gift to be truly cherished. If you do not laugh for a day, if you have not made someone's day happier, if you have not appreciated something good that has happened to you and if you have not felt thankful to be alive, then you have wasted that day of your life on earth. Oh, how I wish I could shout this out from the rooftops! How I wish I can shake everybody on the road and tell them this. But I don't do that as I don't want to be labelled 'crazy'. (Wink wink)

I have met some remarkable people over the last few months and I have made some amazing friends. I have learnt so much, Vaibhav. Such a lot really. I have realised that love and faith can indeed work miracles. I have realised that love and friendship do have a power.

I would be joining a Creative writing course shortly. That is something I have always wanted to do.

I wish I could promise to keep in touch with you. Fact is, I really do not know anymore. I have changed now in such deep ways and am a totally different person from the one you knew. You will not recognise me anymore. I am no longer the same girl you once fell in love with.

Take care—and you will always mean a lot to me. I can never say good bye to you and so I will just say that I will write back if you do.

For the times we have spent together,

Love and laughter

Ankita.

I felt my heart sing as I almost skipped to post the letter to Vaibhav. I felt proud of myself. On the way, I stopped to admire a bunch of yellow chrysanthemums that had just bloomed. I sucked in the air deeply. I rejoiced in the sensation.

And when it began to rain, I smiled in delight, admiring each drop as it fell to the earth.

I was celebrating being alive and there was a strong feeling in my heart that the celebrations would last a lifetime now.

Epilogue

Fifteen years later—what finally happened.

Ankita went on to gain six more academic degrees. Her thirst for knowledge was insatiable. It was as though she could not get enough of reading and as though she could not get enough of academics. One of her degrees included a Masters in Art therapy. Along the way she met a kind sensitive man, fell in love and got married to him. He fully understood what she had gone through and admired her all the more for it. They have a four year old child who is already exhibiting artistic talent. She now lives in Bangalore, and practises as an independent art therapist working with schools as well as conducting sessions for corporate clients. She manages her bipolar disorder with no medication whatsoever thanks to her very supportive spouse and her network of closest friends.

Vaibhav went on to the United States and pursued a Masters degree from the University of Massachusetts and majored in computer science. He and Ankita corresponded for sometime but gradually lost touch. Vaibhav met somebody from his course and they grew closer and are now married. Vaibhav went on to establish his own company in IT and is doing very well for himself and has settled down in the United States of America.

Suvi went on to be the first woman to be on the board of Directors in the multinational she worked for. She excelled professionally and is hailed as one of the biggest business leaders of our times. She is still unmarried and is waiting for Mr.Right.

Dr. Namita now heads the O.T wing at NIMH. She loves her job and would not give it up for anything else in the world.

Dr. Madhusudan has now retired. He went on to establish the first suicide helpline in Kerala. It is manned by volunteers handpicked and trained by him. Since the time it was established it has saved hundreds of lives.

Sagar has set up his own large scale dairy farm at Coonoor in Tamilnadu, India. It also has a large holiday resort with well tended gardens which is much sought after. He started the trend of eco-tourism which took off in a big way and he also won an award from the Goverment of India for his initiative. He is married and his wife gave birth to a set of twins last year and he is the proud father of two cherubic baby boys.

Anuj went on establish an outdoor trekking company which specialises in trekking holidays. He travels regularly with groups to various places like Peru, Nepal and Uganda. He got married but the marriage lasted only three years. He calls himself a footloose and fiancée free bachelor now.

Chaya, Jigna , Uday and Joseph went on to complete their MBAs and are all well employed in various positions in multinationals.

Author's note

This book is a work of fiction but it is based on some real life experiences. However, all names of persons, Institutions and few other details have been changed to protect identities.

The book is not just about bipolar disorder. It is a story of courage, determination and growing up. It is also about how life can take a totally different path from what is planned, and yet how one can make a success out of it. It is a story of faith, belief and perseverance too and charting your own destiny.

Mental health issues are still a big taboo especially in India. In the west, there is more awareness on this condition and it is elevated to almost a status of a 'celebrity disorder' with several people such as Kurt Cobain, Sinead O Connor, Mel Gibson, Axl Rose and Ozzy Osbourne, to name a few, having admitted to have it. In India, people still prefer not to talk about it and even if anybody suffers from it, it is usually hushed up, like anything to do with mental health is.

Bipolar disorder is a serious brain disorder that causes dramatic shifts in moods, energy levels, attitudes and ability to carry out everyday tasks. It is very different from the normal mood changes that everybody goes through from time to time. It develops typically in late adolescence or early adulthood. The symptoms are very severe and it is usually hard to diagnose, as it is not easy to spot when it starts. The symptoms may often seem like very normal personality changes which a person undergoes, in the course of day to day living.

Bipolar disorder can be so severely crippling that that it can result in damaged relationships, poor job or academic performance and even suicide. It has also been associated with creativity. People with this disorder experience intense emotional states which alternate between a 'high episode' called manic episode and it is followed by a 'low episode' called a depressive episode. During a manic state, the person feels overly happy, outgoing and is bursting with high energy levels. Creativity is at an all time high. There is a huge increase in goal directed activities and the person is usually restless and needs very little sleep. The person is very energetic, optimistic and enthusiastic about everything.

In contrast, during a low period, there is an increasing feeling of worthlessness or emptiness which is hard to describe. The person feels exhausted and has trouble concentrating or remembering things and making decisions. There is a loss of interest in everything that the person once enjoyed including sex. Often the person thinks of death and suicide attempts are not uncommon.

There are several variations of bipolar disorder. For more information on these please log on to the website of Nationai Institute of Mental Health (Web site: http://www.nimh.nih.gov) , from which the above information too has been condensed.

In India and China alone, there are at least 12-15 million people who suffer from Bipolar disorder. (Source: Bipolar statistics quoted by the Depression and bipolar support alliance)

The message that I also wanted to convey through this book, is that having a condition like Bipolar disorder does not mean that the person is 'crazy' or a 'lunatic' which are terms which people use without even a second thought. Having a disorder like that does not mean it is the end of the world either. It can be managed in a number of ways and people affected can lead very positive and complete lives.

Writing, by its very nature, is such an intense and a lonely exercise. It was not easy, writing this kind of a book, without getting into the skin of the characters, which would often leave me drained and emotionally exhausted.

This book could never have been written without the support of my spouse Satish Shenoy (who I consider one of my closest friends) and I feel blessed to be married to him. He would completely take over the practical aspects in running the house, would look after the children and would give me my space and time without which I would never have been able to cope with being a full time mother, wife, writer and artist rolled into one. When he finally sat down to read the entire book, I was rewarded when I saw that he was totally engrossed in it and just couldn't stop reading it, till he had completely finished it in just a single sitting. That was a big compliment to me as the biggest critics are usually the ones closest to you.

I also wish to mention the role of one of my closest friends, Ajay Chauhan who was extremely encouraging and supportive.

He would keep sending me mails, asking me when I would write the next chapter and he compelled me to keep writing. He made me feel like I am the greatest writer on Earth. He was there for me throughout, unfailingly when I needed him and he remains a rock-solid, dependable pal. I am grateful and happy to have him in my life.

My closest friend Cherrisa Castellino's help proved invaluable as she read through numerous drafts and re-drafts. I cannot imagine life without her and she remains one of my biggest emotional anchors.

A big thank you to another very dear friend Mayank Mittal whose countless international phone-calls kept me going. He has no idea how much he really helped.

A thank you to all my other friends too (you know who you are)

A special thanks to Dr. Anubhav Naresh too for all the phone-calls and the text messages and of course, the help.

A heartfelt thanks to my blog readers who kept asking me when my next book will be out and telling me that they couldn't wait to read it.

An even bigger thanks to all of you who made my first book a National Best Seller –your encouragement helped.

Thanks to my mother who understands me always and to my two wonderful children Atul and Purvi,who always co-operate when 'Mummy needs to write'.

And also a big thank you to the team at Srishti.

If you have been inspired by this book and if you have enjoyed it, I would consider my task complete.

The world is indeed a better place when there is love, friendship, acceptance and hope. Powered by these, you can indeed overcome anything, including destiny.

Preeti Shenoy
21st December 2010

By the same author

Wake Up, Life is Calling

A sequel to Life is What You Make It

Ankita has fought a mental disorder, been through hell, and survived two suicide attempts. Now in Bombay, surrounded by her loving and supportive parents, everything seems idyllic. She is not on medication. She is in a college she loves, studying her dream subject: Creative Writing.

At last leading a 'normal life', she immerses herself in every bit of it – the classes, her friends, her course and all the carefree fun of college.

Underneath the surface, however, there is trouble brewing. A book she discovers in her college library draws her in, consumes her and sends her into a terrifying darkness that twists and tears her apart. To make matters worse, a past boyfriend resurfaces, throwing her into further turmoil.

Can she escape her thoughts? Will Ankita survive the ordeal a second time around? What does life have in store for her?

Preeti Shenoy's compelling sequel to the iconic bestseller *Life is What You Make It* chronicles the resilience of the human mind and the immense power of positive thinking. The gripping narrative demonstrates with gentle wisdom how by changing our thoughts we can change our life itself.